UNBURIED

ALPHA'S LITTLE PSYCHO
BOOK 2

K.A. BAUER

Unburied (Alpha's Little Psycho 2)
Cover Artwork by K.A. Bauer
Copyright © 2023 K.A. Bauer
All Rights Reserved

Paperback ISBN 979-8-9892840-5-4

Note: This is a work of fiction. Any references to real events, people, or places are used fictitiously. Names, characters, places, and events are products of the author's imagination. Any similarity to real persons, living or dead, is coincidental and not intended by the author.
CIP data for the individual books are available from the Library of Congress

❀ Created with Vellum

TRIGGER WARNING

PLEASE DO NOT PROCEED IF YOU ARE NOT
COMFORTABLE WITH THESE ELEMENTS.
YOUR MENTAL HEALTH IS MORE IMPORTANT
THAN MY BOOK SALES.

Please be advised that this book contains mention or depiction of the following elements which may be upsetting or triggering to some readers.

BDSM

AGE PLAY

CHILD ABUSE AND NEGLECT

SEXUAL ASSAULT

TRAFFICKING

PTSD FLASHBACKS

BULLYING

SUICIDAL IDEATIONS

EXTREME VIOLENCE

EXPLICIT LANGUAGE

UNBURIED

ALPHA'S LITTLE PSYCHO BOOK 2

PROLOGUE

Unburied

<u>Edward</u>
King of the Eastern US Vampires

---

40 Years Ago

Why on earth am I in the deliverance/redneck capital of the cesspit that is Ohio? I know everything east of the Mississippi is technically my territory, but come on... Ohio??? Can we please just nuke it and New Jersey and start over in those two areas? I mean, at least Florida has Orlando tourism to save it, but there is nothing here to salvage this gods forsaken territory except a couple mediocre football teams. They could at least get a hockey team here... that's the only thing that could possibly save this landfill full of the disgrace of humanity.

Touring the territory is something I have to do every twenty years at minimum. If I don't do it, the other supernaturals out there seem to think we vampires are a myth or something. I don't understand it. I've been on this planet for over six hundred years now. My two younger brothers and I have been in charge of what is the modern day contiguous United States of America for the last few centuries after our father decided to retire to Australia...lucky bastard. I can't wait to reach one thousand and get the full protection from the sun.

My uncle finally gave up his rule over modern day Canada after the second World War. My cousins are a bit more hands on than we are...but then again, they don't have Texas, Florida, California, and this unholy waste of space.

Pulling away from Dayton, I head towards the location of the Jameson pack. They've always been pretty remote, and conveniently close to Indiana, so they're usually my last stop in the state. Traditionally, the Alpha there has been very hospitable to me. I'm sure this Alpha...

What's his name again? Alistair... what is it with the old timey names these pretentious wolves like to use?

Anyways, Alistair has invited me to stay for a few days and show me around and go over the updates and changes he set up. For a man of barely forty years, he seems pretty well put together. From what I understand, he just took over after his father had been shot during a hunting accident. Drunk rednecks and rifles don't mix. I never asked if his father was man or wolf when he was shot, but dead is dead, and I sent my condolences as a good king should.

Pulling up to the pack house, I have to say I am impressed at the way they built the town. Most of the homes are spread out with woods in between. The pack house is at the center of the territory, along with the buildings that appear to be an elementary school and a community center, but any humans who end up passing through will only see a few homes along country roads. It is a creative way to discourage uninvited guests and ensure that they aren't seen in their wolf forms. I'll have to remember to let Alpha know that I approve.

Getting out of the car, my blood starts to sing. I have not felt this before in all of my years, but my parents and brothers spoke of it enough for me to know. My fated one is nearby.

While Alistair is introducing me to those present, my mind is only on finding the one for whom my blood is calling out. I don't hear anything he is saying. I just need to find the one fate has decided belongs to me. I feel the sparks when I touch her hand. Meeting her eyes, I see the confusion and happiness quickly replaced by fear. Is my mate afraid of me? That isn't supposed to be.

"And this is Olivia, Russel's mate," Alistair is saying, "These two scamps are their kids, Esther and Carl," he adds pointing out the two children playing with his son in the yard behind him.

"It's wonderful to meet you, King Edward," says this Russel fellow. I nod and try to hide the pure rage I'm feeling inside. This wolf dared to sire children with my fated one and yet he smiles at me... and what a fake smile he has. I want to rip out his intestines with my bare hands and make a necklace out of them, but his daughter has come over to hug her father. I won't hurt a child. He doesn't know how lucky he is.

Alpha Alistair seems to notice something is bothering me, so he excuses everyone else and brings me to his office. With a generous serving of aconite laced whiskey in hand, I take a seat and allow myself to breathe again. I don't really care for the bitter taste, but I can guess the Alpha wants something to actually take an edge off today. I wish there was an alcohol that works on vampires for longer than a minute or two.

"Is everything alright?" he asks. He sees more than others. I'll have to be careful with him. "Did Olivia do something to offend you?"

"She could never offend me," I whisper, forgetting the penchant for overhearing that wolves have.

He gives me a strange look but doesn't say anything. Downing the alcohol in front of me, I push it aside and get down to business.

***

Approximately One Year Later

It has been almost a year since I last set foot in this gods forsaken state. At least this time, I flew in so that I can limit the time I have to spend here in the armpit of America. All I am doing is picking up my fated one and her children and then we will return to my home on the coast. I want to watch the sunrise with her every morning... And wake up to her singing while she cooks dinner each night.

Her children will be accepted as my own, regardless of their status as wolves. We will all be a family together.

I'm not sure why it took her so long to get in touch with me, but I only just now received her letter. In it she stated that three months after I left their territory, she discovered she was with child.

Seeing as how she hadn't lain with her mate since she met me, she knew the babe would be mine. She wrote in her letter that she has been making arrangements to steal away herself and the children once she has healed from the birthing of this pup. From what she told me while I was there, Russel is not the kind of man who will willingly give her up, so she has had to hide our connection and time together. She lied to him and told him the babe would be his, claiming he was drunk when they lain together.

I do not know how or why her letter was delayed. She said in it that she was giving it to the Beta's wife to put in the post. From the date in the letter, it should have been sent months ago. It was only post-marked for last week.

Pulling up to the house that she has spent the last ten years in, I see young Esther sitting on the stoop alone.

"Child, where is your mother?" I ask her gently. "I very much need to speak with her."

There is an anger brewing in this child of barely nine years. She seemed to be very attached to her father when I was last here, and I fear that she will not want to leave with us. My mate will not leave her children behind. She had made that very clear.

"Mother is dead thanks to you and your spawn," she spits at me. "She died months ago. I lost my mother because you are a selfish asshole who only cares about what you want, not what was best for us!"

As she storms up the steps into the house, I let my tears start to fall.

"What of the babe?" I call out before she can close the door.

"My brother and I are the only children of this house!" she screams, slamming the door on me and any semblance of a future that could exist for me now.

———

Almost Sixteen Years Later

I am awakened from my slumber by an unusual feeling. It is like an echo of what I felt with Olivia, but that cannot be. I verified with Alistair. She did die during childbirth sixteen years ago. I should have felt it, but did not for some reason. I wonder often if fate hates me. I already know the gods do.

There are no such things as second chances with fate for a vampire. My brothers are amazed I have even survived this long after losing her, but I am fairly certain the reason is because we never fully claimed each other. She didn't want to alert Russel and lose her children, and I respected that. I wish I had not. I wish every day that I had stolen her and her children away when I left the Jameson pack territory... that I risked the war she wanted us to avoid. I would have won, but she was worried only for the children, the innocents, that would be caught in the crossfire.

I physically shake out the morose feelings that have risen in me, but why am I now feeling this shadow of the blood song? I need to speak to someone who knows more about this than I, so I call my brother, Seamus for some answers. He was lucky enough to find his fated one when he was but sixty-five years of age and they've been together for three centuries now.

Brother? Are you awake? I need your counsel, I send out to him, hoping he has not gone to bed yet. California is three hours behind and it is just past ten in the morning here. It was either him or my father and I can never count on my father to be available anymore. He is thoroughly enjoying his retirement with all of the lethal creatures of the Australian outback.

This had better be important, Seamus responds with a sneer in his tone. *My mate and I were about to have some alone time. It becomes quite rare when there is a toddler in the house.*

I had honestly forgotten Isobel had recently had another babe. This brings the total to ten or so, maybe more. I love my nieces and nephews, but it is getting harder to keep track of them all.

I just need to know something about the blood song when it comes to fated ones, I tell him. *I felt like an echo of what I felt upon meeting*

Olivia, and I do not know what it means. The fates do not give second chances to those of us who meet our mates but do not claim them.

The phone at my bedside rings and I pick up the handset. "You know what this means?" I ask him. There's no need to bother with any greetings.

"How many years has it been since Olivia passed?" Seamus asks me without preamble. He seems both excited and trepidatious.

"Sixteen years to the day," I respond.

There is a weighted silence as I can tell my brother is trying to think of the right way to say something to me. I am going over everything I have learned in my six hundred plus years to try and uncover what he could know that I do not.

"You will want to contact the Alpha," he tells me in a very serious tone. This is the tone he uses when he has to be a king in his own region. "Your bairn lived and has come of age. They belong with us now."

I am stunned into silence. My child is alive? My child has been alive this entire time?

The rage inside of me won't be contained this time. Alistair, Russel, and anyone else who had a hand in keeping me from my child will be feeling my wrath. I slam the handset down onto the receiver and go to my office to get the number of my pilot from my rolodex. I'm flying to Dayton tonight and there will be retribution. I will have my child in my arms before the sun can rise on a new day.

———

"King Edward," Alistair bows, stoically facing me in my anger. "I had no idea the child was yours. Hell, I had no idea she wasn't Russel's until she didn't shift on her thirteenth birthday."

He is taking the time to explain to me and attempt to calm my anger. I can see his reasons behind him. Once again, there are children playing in the yard. They seem to have built a playground of sorts for them to play there... so many more children now. Olivia was right that they needed to be spared from a war, but...

Staring at the children, I start to wonder what she looked like as a child of that age. She... I have a daughter.

"Tell me about her," I demand. I don't know whether to be angry or sad at this point. I've missed her whole life so far. I need to know everything I can about my daughter before I see her. I need to be prepared in case she blames me for abandoning her.

"Elizabeth is very much a copy of her mother physically," he says with a smile. "Everything is like a copy of Olivia, except the eyes... which I can now see she gets from you."

I smile thinking about how amazing it is that our daughter is beautiful like her mother. I truly hope she also inherited her fierce spirit and loving heart and not my cynicism and rage. Seamus and Duncan have regaled me many times over of the joys of raising a teenager and I don't particularly want my only foray into parenthood dealing with a teenage woman with my rage issues.

"What of her upbringing?" I ask. "I know Russel didn't believe she was his. Olivia swore to me she never laid with him after we met."

I need to know what I am going to have to compete with. I'll be taking her away from the only family she's ever known. My daughter is now awakened her vampire powers. She is going to need to be with me and mine for at least a few years until she can control all of her abilities.

"Russel treated the girl differently, yes." Alistair began, "But we assumed it was because he blamed her for Olivia's death. None of us thought of an affair until Lizzie didn't shift."

He is looking uncomfortable talking about my relationship with my fated one like it's a dirty secret.

"Fated mates are never an affair," I state coldly. "Russel was told of our relationship, but he refused to break his arranged mating. Olivia complied for the safety of her existing children as he threatened them to keep her there. She was going to leave him... but

"When I came to collect her and the children, Esther informed me of her death."

Alistair seems to be thinking over something regarding my words. There is a question he wants to ask, but is hesitant to do so...

I don't like to do this, but I pry into his mind to save us some time. I want to see my daughter.

Why didn't he take Liz with him when he was here? I knew he came, but he never stopped in. Why wasn't I informed of any of this?

So, Alistair has spent the last sixteen years as in the dark as I have been. The only reason I didn't take my daughter with me was because Esther told me she died with her mother... didn't she? I have to pull my own memory of that day and revisit it. I have to fight the wave of grief and focus on the words that were said to me.

My brother and I are the only children of this house...

She never told me my child died. She knew Elizabeth was not her father's daughter. I abandoned my daughter. I left her to be raised by a man that I suspect was abusive to my mate, who knew she was not his...

"I need to see her," I stand and turn for the Welling house, but Alistair stops me with a gentle hand at my elbow.

"You need to know something first." He looks over to the children playing in the yard and sighs. "Elizabeth is pregnant."

What in the actual FUCK? The girl just turned sixteen this morning, and yet she is to be a mother?

"Who?" I growl out, rivaling any wolf in existence. The man who had the audacity to lay hands on a fifteen-year-old girl will face the wrath of the entirety of vampire kind...

"She will not say," says a new wolf, coming up carrying one of the boys who had been playing in the yard. "I'm John Sinclair, Esther is my wife and mate. This is our son Connor."

The man looks familiar to me somehow, but then again, most higher ranking wolves do. Six hundred years of seeing the same families in charge of everything means they just all kind of blend together after a while.

"This is my Beta," Alistair indicates towards the man. "His parents retired and moved to Canada to live out their golden years as full wolves."

It's rare for wolves to choose that kind of a life, but some just feel the connection to nature more strongly than others. The Sinclair family is one of them, having their own blessing on their bloodline. They tend to burn out quicker as well.

My attention is drawn back to little Connor in his father's arms. The little boy waves at me and I can see my Olivia in his smile. He is a boy of maybe five years of age and I'm struck again at how I've missed my daughter's youth.

"She is currently in the hospital," John continues. "My father-in-law is a downright nasty drunk with the aconite whiskey and he didn't appreciate Lizzie refusing to give us a name yet again. She's almost ready to give birth to her son, but refuses to have any of us find the father before she can tell him herself."

Apparently, she can't seem to get through to him with the information she has, but we can't get her better information if she doesn't share with us. I wish she would trust us. We're her family...

His thoughts are so loud, I can't help but hear them. But my mind is fixed on one particular of his tale.

"Russel has done this? Put her in the hospital?" I growl again. That necklace is starting to sound better and better.

Connor whimpers so I make sure to gentle my eyes and stance. There is only one thing that can save Russel now.

"Do you like your grandfather, little one?" I ask the boy as he clings to his father.

He shakes his head and hides his face against his father's neck before he mumbles, "Grandpa's a meanie to Lizbef. He hits her and yells a lot and puts me in the dark room when he makes her cry."

My eyes meet Alpha Alistair's. There's no need for a discussion. I know I have his blessing to kill his subordinate. His growl tells me I will have his assistance in this task.

"John, can you watch Alaric until Richard is back?" the Alpha asks.

"I'll keep both boys here," he replies with a bow of his head. "As your Beta, it is my duty to protect the future Alpha heir."

"You had another kid?" I ask as we start the run over to the Welling house.

"Lydia is too old to be birthing new pups, but don't tell her I said that. Alaric is my grandson," he explains. "I really hope the fates let me live long enough to skip over Richard."

At my look of incredulity, he laughs and explains, "I love my son, but he is a narcissistic idiot. He's a decent man, a good husband and father, but would make a terrible Alpha if he doesn't learn to think for himself. He relies too heavily on outside influences."

I'm able to reflect on the Alpha's words for the rest of our run through the woods. I will have to make sure to keep them in mind for the future dealings with this pack since I will be around much longer than any of them. If Richard is such a screw up, perhaps I should make an offer.

"Would you consider relocating the pack at all? Perhaps closer to where I am?" I ask him as we slow down our approach. The house is in view now.

Alistair grunts and gives me a dark look. "This is Jameson land. This has always been Jameson land. You can take what is yours and go, but our blood receives its strength from the land and this is our land."

I can appreciate his dedication to the land of his ancestors, but he's wrong. I won't tell him that, though. A man's pride can only take so many hits in one day. I nod to show him that I accept his answer as we climb the steps.

At the door of the Welling house, we are let in by Carl and pointed to the stairs. It's not difficult to locate the bedroom where Russel is passed out drunk. The boy, or I should say man since Carl is now twenty-one or so, doesn't bother to hide his disgust as he leaves the room, and then the house. He knows what we are going to do here. He just doesn't care. I really have zero regrets for what I'm about to do to this sorry excuse of a man.

As I hold my grandson in my arms, I am torn. Here is a new life, a new prince, but my heart weeps. He is wolf. I can feel it in my blood. He needs pack, not me. He needs his mother, but she is not able to hold him. She didn't make it.

I never got to meet my daughter. I will feel that pain forever. Even as his mother is gone, this tiny babe holds her light inside of him… the same light that shone in my Olivia. Why is it that the mother and daughter both had to die to bring a new life into the world? Why do the fates keep giving to me just to take it all away before I can grasp it?

Is this my punishment for the evil deeds I have done over the centuries? Please, let it not be the case. I cannot stand the thought of my grandson, this beautiful little creature in my arms, paying for my sins.

Ethan... that is what she has named him with her dying breath. Prince Ethan Lewis Sullivan, that shall be his name. Lewis after my own father, who will love to meet him. But that will have to wait. The outback is no place for a baby and I'd prefer he have more protections before he is introduced to the world as a Sullivan. He at least needs to have his wolf.

Ethan is a wolf. I can see it in his mind already. Growing up without a pack will stunt a wolf's growth and can cause insanity, so as King to the region, I make sure that all wolf babes are raised in a pack. He should be good to be with his Aunt and raised alongside his cousin. John seems like a good man and Connor is a beautiful boy who reminds me so much of Olivia.

I haven't seen Esther at all, but I'm sure to have raised such a wonderful boy as Connor so far, she must be the same as her mother. I can think of no other family to raise my grandson until his wolf manifests. If his wolf doesn't manifest, I will take him myself and show him the ways of the vampire. He will know love from both of our people.

Handing my grandson over to Alistair is the hardest thing I've ever had to do. The Alpha has promised me that he will look in on him and keep me updated. I have his blood oath that Ethan will never be mistreated and will be raised as a child of the Beta's family as to not have history repeated with what happened with Elizabeth.

I have his word that if there is any indication of mistreatment, he will bring Ethan to me personally. There is another pack closer to home that I could trust with my grandson. The Alpha there is an idiot, but his son is a good young man and will be a terrific

Alpha when he takes over. I'm sure I could easily find a family there to care for Ethan if it becomes necessary.

Walking away, I pray that Ethan will understand. I will see him again in thirteen years, maybe sooner if I can carve out time for quick stops. I won't let him be abandoned like his mother was. I may not be able to reveal myself to him for his safety, but I will always have someone keeping an eye on him. Alistair knows the power of the blood oath, and with his own son and Beta as witnesses, there is no doubt he will keep it.

Thirteen Years Later

In the grand scheme of things, being delayed four months should not be a big deal. I check my rearview and can barely see over the pile of presents in the backseat. I'm going to be meeting my grandson again for the first time since he was a baby and yeah, I can honestly say I'm hoping to buy his forgiveness. I'm pretty sure he was disappointed when I wasn't there on his birthday. I promised Alpha Alistair I would be, and then time got away from me.

More like a fae issue down in Atlanta keeping me occupied for months when I thought it would only be days. I hate that they have that time difference thing going on inside their mounds. Rip Van Winkle and Thomas the Rhymer are just fairy tales to the humans, but yeah that kinda stuff happens. Twenty minutes to put a stupid prince in his place and explain that he can't just take human babies from hospitals... That wasted twenty minutes of my life was almost six months out here...

I haven't heard from Alistair personally in almost ten years, but the email updates came every year on his birthday with a few pictures of Ethan and his cake. Apparently, the Sinclairs took him in completely and he doesn't know he's biologically not theirs. That was something we discussed a few days after I got home. He didn't want to overstep and change Ethan's last name without my permission, but I agreed that it was safer for him to be a Sinclair. I should have thought about it before I left, but grief makes you miss things.

And that's another reason for the present explosion in my back seat. Nothing like showing up and going, "Hey, kid! I'm your grandfather, and a vampire. Oh and yeah, you're adopted!" That's going to go over real well with a thirteen year old. Seamus just went through this age with Joshua. Apparently, we're just too old to get it, whatever it is. He's a whiz on the computer and we're all over here trying to figure out why we are able to get on the internet without feeling like we're going to puncture an eardrum.

Driving through the Jameson pack territory it's eerily silent. There are no cars, no lights on in any houses, and even some lawns are overgrown. There is a pit in my stomach. Alistair has so much pride in his territory. How could this happen?

I pull out my phone and try to call Alistair. The person who picks up is definitely not the Alpha and I get a young voice in my ear saying, "New phone. Who dis?"

I hang up the call and I pull up my email. I opened the one from Ethan's birthday, but now I see that there is one from the Alpha dated two days after Ethan's birthday. How did I miss this?

```
King Edward,

    It is with the deepest regret that I
must inform you that your grandson has
died. There was a gas leak and Ethan's
alarm triggered the explosion that took
his life and the lives of John and Esther
```

Sinclair. We will be not be holding a funeral due to the tragedy affecting so many of the pack. Please understand.

   -Alpha Jameson

My grandson is dead?

Ethan is gone?

Fire is one of the few ways to kill a vampire, and it will certainly kill a human or wolf.

I drive faster to the Beta house and can't breathe as I pull into the driveway. There is no house left. All that remains is a charred husk, support beams blackened and ready to fall at any moment.

Rage consumes me and suddenly, I am standing in the middle of the wreckage covered in soot. I don't remember getting out of the car. There are no support beams standing anymore. There is no life in this pack anymore. There is nothing here for me to see. It is beyond time to find the Alpha and get some answers.

Climbing back into the car, I write up an email to Alistair to find out where the hell he is and why he lives when my grandson is dead.

Email Undeliverable is the response I receive. He is a dead man.

Three Years Later

A pounding in my chest brings me to my knees. The last time I felt this was thirty-six years ago... There's only one reason I would be feeling this.

Ethan is alive. My grandson is alive. And I have an Alpha to kill.

I have to stop in my search for Joshua. The little shit ran away over eighteen months ago when I announced he's going to be my heir. Seamus will just have to understand. My grandson takes precedence over my nephew…

Like hell will you stop looking for my son! My brother shouts into my head. *Jameson will still be there to kill for quite a while. My son is in danger. I know it and he's somewhere in YOUR territory. Find him or it will be war between us, brother.*

Seamus is right. Joshua is in danger. Ethan is most likely tucked away somewhere safe. It was likely my enemies found out about him and set the fire. Alistair was keeping him safe and keeping me away. He'll contact me soon, right? I mean, if Ethan didn't get his wolf like his mother, he would have to be sent away, right?

Either way, I need answers…

Not before you have my son!

Damn little brothers! Alistair better hope he has some good answers for me. I'm really not in the mood.

1

Unburied

Ethan

Captain's log... Scratch that.

Ethan's log... today's date? Who knows... Every day is blending into the next. The wonder and joy of freedom has turned to boredom. Like, I know that shit was bad for me before and all, but being treated nice and everything is just so blah...

Here I am, sitting in a college classroom and it's just so... meh. Don't get me wrong. I'm psyched to be able to even go to school like this, but this professor is just so freaking dull. Every single class is a struggle to stay awake while he drones on and on about the fathers of modern psychology. I only took intro to psychology as a compromise with Connor.

He wants me to do therapy. I don't want any more strangers all up in my business, especially of the d-word variety. Me and docs are a big ole NOPE. Ric suggested this class so that I can "better understand what psychology is so I can make an informed decision."

If psychology is falling asleep in a classroom he's spending an arm and a leg for me to be in, then yeah I'd say my choice to not go to therapy is valid.

I'm not saying I don't want to talk about everything that happened to me. Keeping quiet isn't something I ever wanted or want to keep doing going forward. I've uncovered too many secrets already... but that trauma shit gets buried deep in you. Every time I've tried to open up to Connor or Ric, they look so broken and disappointed that I shut down again. I hate hurting them, so I stopped trying to tell them about things that bother me.

Max is really my only confidant. We don't say it out loud, but he knows some of what I feel. Not everything, thank the gods, but he knows enough to know I don't want or need to see horror or pity or anger. I just need someone to listen and acknowledge that it really happened and I'm really here now... that this isn't all just a dream even after all of these months. But even Max can't understand it all. When I forget and let him see, I feel the gap between us getting wider. I'm even too fucked in the head for him sometimes...

You know who this professor reminds me of? That teacher in the one movie from like forty years ago about the kid who skips school. Same voice. Same mannerisms. Man, now I want to pull out my phone and watch eighties movies instead of sitting through the rest of this hour. How long have I been here tonight?

Fifteen minutes...

Screw this. I'm ditching. The movie made me do it... That's my excuse and I'm sticking to it. It's not like I'll get counted as absent. This professor takes roll at the beginning of the classes, unlike my Advanced Anatomy prof who randomly selects half the names for roll call in the beginning and the other half at the end of class. Sometimes, he'll call people twice just to make sure they stayed for the whole class. Love the class, hate him.

Anyways, leaving the class, Mr. Monotone doesn't even glance my way. I don't really care if Freud slept with his mother or whatever he's talking about. I'll just read the book to catch up. Right now, my biggest hurdle is ditching the guard dog I'm saddled with. Today, I have Thing One, also known as Seb, as my not so faithful companion. Nothing wrong with the guy, but we both agree Ric needs to chill out with the guard duty. He and his brother, Bastien, are my usual watch dogs for the night class shift since the other warriors don't seem to like me too much after Christmas.

Ever since I woke up after the whole Gathering debacle, I haven't had a moment alone outside of the house. If I go to the store, I have a guard. If I go for a walk, I have a guard. If I check the freaking mail, I have a guard. Only good thing about having them around over the last few months was that I didn't have to lug everyone's Christmas presents through the mall. I had my built-in luggage trolleys. I think that was the last straw for most of them.

I honestly didn't mean to buy as much as I did. When Ric got the credit card bill last month, I thought he was going to be the first werewolf ever to die of shock. I didn't know a person could change colors like that without being strangled.

I apologized and even offered to let him return all of the things he bought for me to help pay for it, but he refused. Instead, he took away the card that doesn't have a limit and replaced it with one that limits me to only one thousand at a time. "For emergencies" is what he told me. Well, coffee is an emergency right now.

Thing One is nowhere to be found outside of the classroom. Daddy isn't going to be happy about that, but I'm super duper excited. This means I can get the coffee I like and not get a lecture about it being sugary milk with a dash of coffee. I mean, morning coffee needs to be dark like my soul. Just kidding. I need my creamer. But nighttime coffee is dessert. I'd get it iced, but early

February is just too cold for iced anything unless I'm in my jammies under a blankie.

Making my way across the quad to reach the coffee shop, I ignore the stupid beta idiots from the local pack cat-calling all the women walking by them. Who in their right mind would fall for dumbass dudebros like them? I put them out of my mind as the scent of the liquid ambrosia is wafting over to me. It's calling to me…

"Leave me alone, asswipe!" It's a woman's voice cutting through the fog created by the siren song of the coffee. Ignore it, Ethan. You want your coffee, right? Just ignore it…

"Get your fucking hands off me, you neanderthal!"

Damnit! Fucking hero complex bullshit. I blame comics.

"You pencil dicks can't get anyone with your looks, so you use force?" I shout in their direction, trying to distract them enough that the lady can get away. Most of them look my way, but one of them still has his hands on the woman.

"Because it's obvious your personalities can't carry you either," I continue as I turn towards them instead of the heavenly nectar. They are really not going to like ruining my plans if the coffee shop runs out of muffins before I can get in there. The night class students go crazy for the clearance baked goods at the end of the night and for once I have a decent shot at a double chocolate muffin.

"Beat it, twinkie," says a chubby frat bro looking douche canoe. Popped collars should have stayed out of style when the eighties ended. I recognize him. This guy is in my Econ class. He's one of those guys that his daddy (not Daddy, at least I don't think he swings that way) bought his way into a college education. Hell, I think he bought his high school diploma as well, maybe even kindergarten…

"Shit! The bitch got away!" yells another of the dudebros.

Since my job is apparently done, I turn back towards the coffee shop. I know better than to turn my back to potential enemies. I'm not stupid... but coffee... and muffins...

2

Unburied

Yeah, today is apparently the day for stupid decisions cuz now I'm coming awake on a concrete floor somewhere that smells like sawdust. I rub the back of my head where there is a decent goose egg formed. You know how hard you have to hit a shifter for a visible mark to remain after this long? Daddy is not going to be happy at all about this.

Daddy? You hearing me?

And... radio silence. Shit.

Where in the hell did they take me that I'm out of range? Everywhere that is wolf territory, neutral, or the shopping district is within range of the pack. So unless Ric went out somewhere in the opposite direction, he should be able to hear me... unless he isn't answering because he's mad at me. I did disobey him and ditch Seb at school...kinda regretting that now.

Looks like I'm on my own for this rescue operation. At least I remembered to put my backpack on all the way, so I still have it on my back. Reaching in, I dig around to locate Mr. Whiskers in the depths. It's time to break out Stabby... but first I have to find him. Why do I have so much crap in here for one night class?

The beta wolves are all in another room. They put me in some sort of an office it looks like. I can hear them arguing on what to do with me, but I tune it out. I can't seem to find Mr. Whiskers in my bag. He should be in here! Now that we've been reunited, he doesn't leave me... ever. He needs to be in here!

I dump the contents of my bag out on the floor before my panic turns into whines. I don't want to alert the idiots that I'm awake until I'm armed. Everything is scattered on the floor, but there's no Mr. Whiskers. There's no Stabby. I'm defenseless...

You have me, my wolf reminds me.

One omega wolf against three betas isn't exactly ideal odds, I tell him. Could I take them down? Probably... maybe? I don't really want to have to find out. I'd much rather take them on in this form.

Looking around the room, I see nothing that can help me... unless...

There's a letter opener on the desk. Those things are never sharp enough, but it might be enough. Picking it up, I run my thumb across the blade. The itch I feel tells me it's silver and surprise surprise, there is a decent edge on the blade. It's almost like it was made to be inconspicuous to be used against werewolves.

I won't kiss a horse or whatever the saying is...

Letting out a light cough, I prepare myself for some fun. I'm not going to get any playtime again for a while. I'm in so much trouble now... gotta take advantage of this and make it really interesting.

Every single Tuesday for the last five weeks has been torture. After dinner, I send Ethan off to his night class with a guard. Then I wait anxiously for the next two, sometimes three, hours until my boy comes back through that door. The class is only an hour, but Ethan loves his treats, so I allow him to indulge in the coffee shop on campus after class. It's safe enough and I will never again make the mistake of getting between my Blue and his coffee.

The university is located in the Heartstone pack. The only times I've been in the pack have been to take Ethan to or from class. I try not to associate with Alpha Bennet much considering his affiliation with the vampires. I can't blame him, since his father is the reason he's stuck in an alliance with them, but the only good vampire is a truly dead vampire.

Wait, that's not true. From the documents Ethan gathered from his "secret room" there was a lot of mention of good relations and a blood oath between my grandfather and the vampire king. From what I read, they were at least on good terms, if not outright friends... and my father framed this king for his father's murder. I still don't understand why my dad had to kill my grandpa...

Seeing Thing One's face lighting up my phone screen, I swipe up. Max got us all referring to the twins as the Dr. Seuss characters so we use the drawings as their ID pictures. I wonder what my boy is requesting of him now. Seb hates the smell of coffee so I can only imagine what hell my little bluebird is putting him through right now.

"What's up, Seb?"

"Alpha, I swear I was only gone a second..."

WHAT THE FUCK? That is not the way to initiate this conversation. I knew we should have waited longer to send him to school. Online colleges are just as good and it's the same degree.

"There better not be a hair out of place on his pretty ginger head," I snarl into the phone.

"See, the thing is... I don't know," he tells me. Before I can rip him a new asshole, he continues, "I had to take a leak and little man was fighting falling asleep at the table. I swear I thought he was asleep, so I ran to the bathroom two doors away. I don't know how he managed to get out so quick. It was thirty seconds tops!"

My warriors still don't know the full extent of Ethan's speed yet. Until we find out how many of his quirks are due to his being omega or due to something done in the lab, we don't want to encourage anyone to push another to their limits for some extra speed boost.

"There's another problem," Seb says, breaking into my thoughts. What the hell else could be a problem?

"I found Mr. Whiskers at the edge of the quad, near the coffee shop."

My heart skips a beat. So, Ethan is missing and he doesn't have his teddy. He doesn't have Stabby. He is unarmed and missing. My boy is in danger...

FIND MATE, my wolf growls at me.

No shit, Sherlock. I pull up my phone and open up the find my friends app. After the chase to Ohio last summer, we both agreed to have the apps on our phones and to always keep the phones on. I've periodically checked in on Ethan during class, so I know he doesn't turn it off... ok so more than periodically. I may have stalked his location consistently when he first started classes this semester...

But I'm not seeing him at all right now. The phone had a full charge when he left the house. Even with his penchant for watching movies instead of paying attention in class, the phone wouldn't be dead until well after he gets home. Either his phone is broken or he's somewhere with no signal... neither situation sits well with me.

My boy is lost... again.

He was taken from me... again.

I'm spiraling out and don't even realize I've crushed my phone. It's completely obliterated. I stare at the remains of what used to be an expensive piece of technology in my hands for what feels like an eternity. My world has ended...

3

Unburied

Ric

"Why is Seb texting me asking me to make sure you don't kill him?" Connor asks as he comes into the office.

I look up at him with tears in my eyes, "Ethan is missing, and Mr. Whiskers was left behind."

Immediately, my Beta does his sight trick. It's still super freaky to see his eyes glaze over with gold every time he does it. He turns a bit pale before his eyes return to normal and he's racing for the trash can.

His reaction could mean something really good or really bad. I can't really make a judgment call on it when it comes to my little psycho. He truly did become a master at maximum damage without causing death. It's not like we didn't have enough "volunteers" for him to practice on after the Gathering in July. Those that remained of my father's and Mrs. Sinclair's lackeys were dealt with quite fairly. They all received punishment equal to their role in what happened. Most did not survive after Max took his turn. I handled what was left.

Once Connor is positive that his stomach is no longer trying to escape his body through his mouth, he looks at me with a half smile and says, "Well, good news is he's not hurt. And he's having fun."

I brace myself. "The bad news?"

"A vampire came into the room…" he says, flinching at the roar of my wolf.

"Vampires took my mate?!"

He gives me a look that is telling me I need to be patient, but then Connor's phone starts ringing with Ethan's ringtone. The boy fell in love with the song Radioactive by Imagine Dragons and so he insists that it is HIS ringtone on everyone's phone. He answers immediately and puts the phone on my desk, speakerphone already on.

"Little brother, tell us you're alright," he says.

Before Ethan can respond, I add, "Blue, you better have a good explanation or your ass is going to be so very red tonight."

The chuckle on the other end of the line is not Ethan.

"Who is the owner of this phone to you that you would openly say such things?" the stranger asks.

"He is my mate!" I growl at the phone. "And you taking him is tantamount to war, bloodsucker!"

"Excuse him," Connor interrupts, slapping me upside the head.

"The Alpha is a bit overprotective of Ethan after everything he's been through. I believe there was an incident on campus that may have carried over and we thank you for finding my brother. We appreciate any assistance you could give him until we can get there to pick him up. Can you please give us an address? We'll head over right away and get him out of your hair."

Connor, always the diplomat. He never had the hatred against the vampires, even though his mother tried to drill it into everyone... my father as well. When I asked my Beta about it, he just replied that he once met the vampire king and he was a nice man who tried to save Elizabeth. I only recently found out that Elizabeth was Ethan's mother who died in childbirth.

Connor doesn't even remember that she was his aunt. He only remembers her as a nice lady who stayed at his grandpa's house before his grandpa died. The old Welling house became Carl's house and now it sits empty... as it should. I don't know if Connor even knows that she died...

"Ah, and who are you? I can assume you are the Beta of the pack by the way you handle your Alpha." The voice on the other end of the phone is not familiar, but there is something in the tone of the voice that is tugging at me. I can't put my finger on it.

"Ethan is my little brother and I really would like to bring him home as soon as possible," Connor replies, obviously trying to not reveal how much he is panicking. His body is taught, but he's doing a good job of keeping his voice even. The vampire hasn't said yet that he will actually return Ethan.

"Ah, so Conman... stands for Connor, does it?" the voice asks. "Connor Sinclair... I have known your family for a few generations. You have nothing to fear from me."

That's news to me. Since when did the Sinclairs associate with vampires? Connor looks just as perplexed as I do.

"Your *brother* is currently showering in the locker room of the warehouse. He made a terrible mess of my office," the voice pauses to chuckle. "I truly hoped the temper would have skipped a few generations, but oh well. I will text you the address. He should be done by the time you get here."

We both watch as the alert comes up on the phone showing a text has been received.

"I will be waiting. It will be good to see you again, Connor."

As the vampire disconnects, I open the text to reveal the address. Ethan wasn't just taken to just any warehouse. He was taken to the heart of the vampire headquarters. I'll just have to swallow my pride and play nice for the night to pick him up…

Connor collapses into my chair and starts to chuckle. When he looks up, the chuckle becomes a full on laugh. I wish he'd let me in on the joke. At my raised eyebrow, he gathers his breath enough to get out, "only Ethan would end up creating a crime scene in the office of the fucking vampire King of the Eastern United States…" And he's back to the hysterical laughing.

My night just got a hell of a lot worse.

4

Unburied

<u>Ethan</u>

Ok this letter opener is no Stabby, but I like it a lot.

Really, really a lot.

Think anyone would notice if it slipped into my backpack on the way out of here? I'm sure no one would care. I mean, you can get letter openers anywhere, right? And silver ones have to be popular. I'm pretty sure I saw a bunch when I was doing the Christmas shopping back in December. I'm like eighty seven percent certain of it.

The door opening has me spinning around, almost too fast. I barely catch myself on the edge of the desk before I fall down only to see the door closing. That's weird.

Was it a backdraft thingy with the outside door opening?

Did another friend of the douche patrol show up?

Or did I miss one and I'm going to have to prepare to take on more?

Pulling my backpack out of the filing cabinet I stuffed it in, I dig out my phone to call Daddy. I'm going to at least need Max's help with cleanup here, but I'd rather have Ric here in the event of more fighting. I'm tired and want Mr. Whiskers and my jammies.

I don't like that Mr. Whiskers wasn't here with me.

I swear I hear the door again, but as I turn back around to look at it, the door is shut just like before. It's kind of starting to freak me out a bit. Well, since today seems to be a day of bad decisions, I might as well go for broke.

The door is opening and closing on its own... be the dumb white person in the horror movie, Ethan. Go check out the strange noise and end up getting eaten by a bloodthirsty monster.

Ew... That isn't a thought I wanted popping into my head.

I don't want death by being eaten. Would I come back whole or have to wait for all of my pieces to come back together on their own? Would I just poof up inside of the thing and explode it? Or reincarnate in its shit?

Ugh. Time to stop stalling.

Before I can grab for the handle it turns. The door opens to reveal a man that my nose is telling me is something is familiar with him. And something weird is going on with my body. It's like seeing this guy feels like how I felt around subject number twenty-three in the lab.

Oh...

He's a vampire, too. That must be the reason.

What was twenty-three's name again? Sully. Was that it?

This vampire is staring at me like he's seen a ghost. I don't know what's up with that.

Oh wait, I made a mess. Didn't think vamps would have a problem with blood.

Behind him, I see two big burly enforcer type dudes bent over a couple of barrels losing whatever is in their stomachs. Funny... I didn't know vampires could hurl like that.

This guy in front of me keeps staring. It's kind of freaking me out, but at the same time I'm tempted to give him a hug. It's all very confusing.

You'll learn how to block in time, little one.

FUCK!

So, he's got that little trick, too. I have a hard enough time not broadcasting when I'm stressed and I don't even have Mr. Whiskers to keep me grounded and this guy keeps looking at me like I'm a puppy he lost and then found years later.

That isn't a bad way to put it, Ethan. Go get showered and I will call your people to come get you. Who should I call?

He takes the phone out of my hands since I'm just standing there slack jawed and unmoving. He holds it up to my face to unlock the screen. When the screen unlocks, it reveals the photo of me, Jackie, Mr. Whiskers, and Tony sitting in a blanket fort we made out of the living room after Thanksgiving dinner.

That was an epic day...

Wait a second...

That actually worked to unlock the phone?

Facial recognition works even when I'm covered in blood and guts and... Yeah, I don't really want to know what else. A shower sounds really good. Then, I'll worry about the potential security risks of relying on my face to open the phone. I don't have any secrets, but still - not as safe as I thought.

A name? I doubt you want to come home with me, at least not yet.

This guy is a little forward. I mean he's good looking and all but there's a bit of a squick factor that I can't define when it comes to thinking about him in that way.

Yuck!

Call my Daddy. He's number one in my emergency contacts. If he doesn't answer, just go down the list.

At his quizzical look, I grab my backpack and head towards the door labeled "Locker Room" to take a shower. I don't even bother to undress. I don't have any clean clothing to put on anyways, so I turn on the water and step right under after making sure my bag is far enough away to not get wet, but still in my line of sight.

I trust the talky vampire dude, but not the barfers. Plus, I don't know if these vampires are going to hold this against me or Ric. That wouldn't be fair. Those dumbass betas are all from the Heartstone pack.

Don't you mean were? the talky vampire interrupts my thoughts. Privacy apparently needs an update with more than just the phone.

No. I mean are. I send back to him. *They aren't dead. I'm not allowed to kill.*

I get a distinct feeling of shock and a bit of queasiness before I can tell he completely severs our mind connection. It never gets old the first time someone realizes I do what I do but don't kill. I can even make vamps toss their cookies. I mean it was funny watching Max run from the basement when he brought me the cheese grater, but today feels like more of an accomplishment.

As my giggles die down, I realize my thumb has found its way into my mouth. Nope! This is NOT the time or place to let that happen. I force the little side of me down as far as I can. I can regress when I get home, if I get home. The talky vampire seems to be nice enough to send me home, but he might ask for a ransom or some sort of compensation. I really should have figured out where I was before making a mess like that.

I didn't think this whole wet clothes thing through, either. It might not be Ohio February where the outside temperature is like fifteen degrees Fahrenheit, but thirty degrees with wet clothes at night still sucks. It's rare, but knowing my luck, I'd come down with a cold or something... first wolf to die of pneumonia or some shit like that.

Shutting off the water, I turn around and am surprised to see a towel and some clothing folded next to my bag, with a pair of flip flops underneath. Again with the kissing horses thing... I peel away my soaked, and still kinda bloody, clothing and realize I missed some chunks of shithead number two. He was the blonde, I think...

After my second shower, I manage to towel off and pull on the clean clothes without any more delays. I don't think where we are is too far from the pack, so Daddy should be here soon. I mean, how hard could they have hit me, really? I'm healed already so I'm not worried about that. I'm worried about Daddy.

He really doesn't like vampires, so I need to make sure I'm out there when he gets here. After about two steps, I decide that I hate flip flops, so I ditch them and go out barefoot. I'll heal the frostbite if it happens. I prefer that to the pain between the toes.

Ric

Sitting in the backseat of my own car has become a bit of a habit now. I always want to hold my boy, so the only time I drive anymore is when I'm by myself or just taking Jack somewhere. He was so mad that I wouldn't let him come with us to get Ethan. It's bad enough my mate is with the vampires, I refuse to let them have access to my little brother as well.

As we pull up to the address that was texted to Connor, Max turns around to face me and ask, "So what's the play, Bossman?"

I can smell more than five vampires in the area, but only see the one sitting on the guardrail, swinging his legs like he doesn't have a care in the world. Figures, they don't take us seriously...

Patience, my wolf whispers to me. *This one has power enough to crush us alone.*

The guy is barely six foot and skinny as a twig. There's something about the way he's sitting that reminds me of Ethan, but that's just because I'm not seeing my bluebird here and I need to see him.

"Stay on guard, but don't leave the car unless Ethan is in danger," I tell Max.

"Uh, Ric?" he starts. "You do remember that little dude can't die, right?"

He's ducking away from me like he expects a hit. He deserves one for that comment.

Climbing out of the car, I tell him, "I've seen it twice now and never want to see it again. He doesn't get injured, period."

I maintain eye contact with Max until he gives me a mocking salute. Shaking my head, I start to walk away. What ever happened to respect? Yeah, he's one of my best friends, but damn it's difficult dealing with two smart asses all of the time.

Connor is already making the introductions for me. I really hate vampires. Why couldn't it have been another pack that took Ethan? Or even more humans? Vampires are just so... evil.

"And this is our Alpha, Alaric Jameson," Connor says indicating to me. I guess I have to play diplomat to get my boy back. I try to smile, but I'm pretty sure it comes off as a sneer judging by the look my Beta is giving me.

"Alistair's chosen heir," the vampire says. I missed his introduction. "It's a shame you lost him so early and his plans for the pack didn't come to fruition."

His plans? What plans? How in the fuck does this bloodsucker know anything about my grandfather's plans? I'm pretty sure the vampire is reading my face when he continues.

"Alistair provided me with a very detailed plan of exactly where he was going to take the Jameson pack from the turn of the millennium into the start of your time as Alpha." He leans in to pretend to whisper the next part to us. Even his theatrical delivery is reminding me of Ethan. I need my boy. "He never intended your father to play a role at all. Richard was... let's just say his pride was more important than the pack to him."

I take about three stumbling steps back. I'm a bit flabbergasted at what I'm hearing. My grandfather wanted *me* as his heir, not my father? My grandfather had plans for the pack that my father ignored? Our pack was on good enough terms with this vampire when I was a child that he and my grandfather spoke often? None of this is making any sense to me.

You will understand in time, boy. Your grandfather loved you very much and foresaw the disaster that your father would be as an Alpha. From what I have seen these last six years, he was very much right.

Shit. This vampire can do Ethan's little mind trick. I need to know he's ok. He hasn't reached out to me at all since we've been here and my wolf is incredibly on edge with all of the unseen vampires surrounding us. Hell, he hasn't reached out himself since he was taken from the school. I need to see him NOW.

The door of the warehouse slams open and we all turn to see what the commotion is, in various degrees of readiness for an attack. There is no attack coming. There is my Blue, looking sheepish as all hell when he gently closes the door, revealing a sizeable dent in the side of the building.

It looked heavier than it is, he broadcasts to us all with a shrug. As he walks over, I can see him struggling to keep his hands at his sides. Oh he's very close to regressing. I need to get him home so that he doesn't need to worry about these enemies seeing him in such a vulnerable state. I'd hate to have to kill some of them and start a war.

"There is no need for violence, young Alaric," the vampire says without looking away from Ethan. He's staring at him like a doting parent looks at their child. Just great, the local vampires want to adopt my mate. That's just my luck.

5

Unburied

"Thanks for the towel and clothes, Mr. Vampire Dude," Ethan says as he comes up to us all. "I didn't really want to have to be in this cold in wet clothes and my wolf doesn't really like being open with himself around people he doesn't know."

The vampire chuckles at Ethan's gratitude... or maybe at the cheeky yet totally in character show of respect? I'm honestly amazed sometimes at how my boy can be totally sincere and yet so downright rude. I guess if a goddess lets you get away with it, you wouldn't be inclined to stop.

Connor speaking interrupts my train of thought. I am aching to get my boy home. I don't like being in enemy territory with him, regardless of how nonchalant they have been about him being here.

"Ethan, this is King Edward of the Eastern US Vampire Kingdom. You might not want to call him dude," he is trying to hide his smile while introducing the two officially. The name and title mean nothing to Ethan at all. He's looking at his brother as if waiting for him to get to the important part.

"It is alright, son," Edward says to Connor. "He will hopefully come to know me in time."

My wolf growls at that. There's no way that my little bluebird will spend ANY more time with vampires. They are evil and sadistic and conniving and...

I see your father poisoned your mind quite extensively.

"Stay out of my head, bloodsucker!" I snarl at him.

Connor looks aghast. Ethan looks surprised and... hurt. He's usually a bit turned on when I get all growly around him, but how did that hurt him?

Blue? What did I do? Are you hurt by what I said? I like you in my head. It's the vampire I don't like, not the mind thing. I'm sending as much reassurance to my boy as I can, but he's looking on the verge of tears. How did I hurt him so badly with that? I just want to make it better. I want to get him home and we can snuggle and I'll give him all the sweets he wants. As long as those tears don't fall, I'll give him anything.

"You might want to learn all of the facts before you run your mouth, you damn prick," says a voice from behind us.

I spin around only to see another vampire sitting on the hood of my car. Max is still sitting in the drivers seat, seemingly without a care in the world. Well, I did say not to get out or move unless Ethan was threatened, but come on... letting a filthy bloodsucker sit on my car? We are going to have words later.

Before I can even formulate a plan, Ethan pushes past me and tackles the vampire into the windshield. Thank the gods I upgraded to the bulletproof glass. The impact would have shattered a regular one. Max is already out of the car, but just stands at the open door looking torn. There is a need to protect Ethan, but we also all want to let him have his own power as well. We never take a fight away from him. He deserves to be able to fight his own battles...

But hold up... he's laughing? Why is my boy laughing? I can see now they aren't fighting. They're hugging?!

My wolf is grumbling, but I hold back his growl. I'm so very confused right now.

<u>Ethan</u>

He isn't dead?! Sully isn't dead! They told me he ran away. I didn't believe them. They actually told me the truth. I wasn't lied to for once? He got out. He escaped. He did what I couldn't. The small spark of shame sinks in and I can finally pull back enough to let us both catch our breath.

"How are you alive?" I ask him as we slide off the hood of Daddy's car. He loves this car and is going to be very mad that there's a pretty big dent now... But Sully is ALIVE and HERE. I'm so freaking happy!

"It wasn't easy and I was hurt pretty badly," he says to me.

They tried to take my head off to stop me, but I took theirs instead. He grins at me when he sends that to my head. He's the first person who I was ever able to have the mind to mind conversations with. I used to think he was in there because he was running from something else. Apparently that something else was over by the time he ran.

"How are YOU alive?" he asks me, glancing back at my family behind me with nervous eyes. "You get your rescue from your big brother? Get your kisses from his best friend?"

I push him over playfully. Sully is the only person aside from Shaun from middle school that I ever told about my feelings for Ric. I never asked how old he is, but Sully feels like he's around my age, maybe a few years older but not much.

"Joshua, quit teasing him," snaps the old vampire dude... Edward, right? Yeah I think that's his name. And as for the old, he doesn't look a day over thirty or so, but there's something there that tells me he's freaking ancient.

"Of course, Uncle Edward," Sully, no Joshua, says with a bow. It's like we just jumped back into some old timey movie or something. Being all formal and stiff doesn't work for me, so I decide to just be me and loosen things up a bit.

"Sorry, Gramps. Etiquette and me just don't mix so I don't mind Sully being a bit of a dick," I say over my shoulder.

At the sudden intake of breath from all of the vamps in the area, and man there are a lot of them, I realize I may have gone too far with my loose tongue. I keep forgetting that this guy is a stranger and he's a freaking king and all. He feels almost familiar and it's really confusing but if I dwell on it, I'm just going to get stressed out... er... more stressed out.

"No disrespect meant, Sir," Connor says into the silence, covering my ass yet again. "Ethan didn't exactly have the best instruction on how to be around other people."

Well isn't that a nice way to say, "*My brother was isolated, tortured, then sold to a lab for experiments for pretty much his entire life and was only ever treated like a person by like five people in the whole entire existence of this universe.*"

And damn, now I'm pissed and sad and want Mr. Whiskers. I lost Mr. Whiskers...

6

Unburied

Ethan

I didn't even realize I sat down on the ground, but Daddy's arms are around me and my knees are wet. Am I crying? Why am I crying? Where is Mr. Whiskers? This is his job. He's failing at his job... No. I failed him. I lost him again. I don't deserve his help. I should have never made the deal. I shouldn't be here at all...

NEVER say that again!

My head snaps up at the command in my head from the vampire dude Eddie. Edward. I need to at least try to be respectful. He could kill Connie and Max and Daddy just for me being brought here.

I didn't want to come here. I only ever cause trouble. Why the fuck does anyone want me around? I should have just let them do what they wanted. Now there's a mess and it's all my fault that Daddy is going to die like his father and Jackie will be all alone... it's all my fault. It's always my fault.

"I think it's time you take the little one home," he says to

Connor. It sounds like he's trying to hold back his anger. I don't want him to be angry at them. It's my fault.

Ric picks me up and starts heading for the back door of his car. Max opens the door for him, so that Ric can set me down and buckle me in. I'm in the car now, my thumb is in my mouth and I don't care. Max gets himself situated in the drivers seat and makes eye contact with me through the mirror. I can see the concern in his eyes, but he keeps it off his face. I appreciate it. He doesn't pity me. Or...if he does, he doesn't ever let me see it.

Connor and Daddy are talking to the old vampire dude and Sull... Joshua. I could hear what they're saying if I really want to, but I don't. I don't care. I just want Mr. Whiskers. I need to apologize for leaving him.

He shouldn't forgive me. I was wrong to lose him. If I can't take care of Mr. Whiskers, how am I supposed to be a papa one day? I'm going to be stuck with this damn deal forever just like she wanted. I can't give Ric what he needs. I need to find a way to set him free so that he can have his heirs and continue the pack. I can't be his mate anymore. I only ever hurt him.

I don't remember Daddy and Connor getting into the car. I don't remember the drive back home. I don't remember going upstairs to our bedroom. The next thing I remember is seeing Mr. Whiskers sitting in his spot on our bed. He forgives me.

Daddy holds us tight as I sob out my thanks that Mr. Whiskers isn't mad at me for losing him again. I'm so happy that my first and oldest friend hasn't abandoned me. He'd be right to do so. I so don't deserve him.

Ric

Shit! Something just triggered my boy. I don't even know what it was that set him off. We rarely know until he comes out of his panic attacks and even then, sometimes he can't remember what the exact thing was. All of us want him to get into therapy, but I also understand his mistrust of doctors. I'm so lost on what to do to help him through all of this.

Every time he has one of these attacks, it shreds me inside a bit more. I'm so raw on the inside, but I don't know what to do about it. I'm the Alpha. I'm his Daddy. I'm supposed to be strong enough to handle everything. I need to be able to shoulder it all. I'm failing him so much, but I'm so lost on what to do for him. How do I help him and still get to keep him? He needs someone so much stronger than I am.

Right now, the only thing I can do is hold him as he's sobbing and screaming on the ground. King Edward appears to be really disgusted by my boy's display of weakness, but I don't give a flying fuck what this asshole thinks. Ethan has been through more than anyone should ever have to deal with, and he's still here. He's still fighting. No one has the right to look down on my boy in any way... not while I breathe.

When Edward suggests we get Ethan home, I don't waste any time. I lift him in my arms to carry him to the car. He just feels so fragile like this, it's killing me. Being so powerless is like a poison to my soul, but I'll do anything to help him. I would do anything, promise anything, if I could only find a way to cure him of these episodes.

After depositing my mate safely in the car, I return to do the diplomatic thing and say our goodbyes to the vampire king. As much as I hate them, at least he has been decent enough. He gave Ethan clothes when he didn't have to. He assisted my boy and even reunited him with a friend.

Speaking of this Josh fellow, he's just standing behind King Edward, his entire being surrounded by an aura of shame. It's obvious he blames himself for my boy's breakdown, but I have no intention of putting his mind at ease. For all I know, he ran and left Ethan to rot in that lab. He deserves to feel everything, same as we all do for failing my sweet little bluebird.

"Alpha Alaric, a word please?" the king requests while gesturing that we should step to the side, away from prying eyes. I nod for Connor to join Ethan and Max in the car, and that Josh guy zips away. Damn, apparently vampires can be faster than Ethan's wolf. That's a good thing to be aware of. Know your enemy and all that.

"There is something you need to be aware of when it comes to your mate," Edward starts with a sigh.

"What could you possibly tell me about my mate that I don't know?" I ask heatedly. "I've known him since the day he was born. I'm the one who has spent every night for the last six months at his side. I'm the one who shares his dreams, his nightmares, his memories."

How DARE this vampire think he knows more about my mate than I do. My wolf growls in agreement.

I know things you don't because you were a babe yourself when he was born. I was the first one to hold him after his mother passed. I lifted him from her cooling body because the nurses weren't willing to touch him or his mother once the birthing was complete. You damn wolves and witches and faeries thinking anything dealing with us is tainted, cursed or evil... it's a damn miracle I didn't destroy the hospital that day.

What the hell is he on about? What the hell does Ethan's mom have to do with vampires? And why wouldn't they touch Ethan?

The bastard is looking at me like I'm an idiot. What the fuck am I supposed to be figuring out here? What does my boy have to do with filthy bloodsuckers?

If it wasn't for the fact that I know he loves you, I wouldn't let my grandson anywhere near you or your damned dysfunctional, bigoted, and speciest pack.

Grandson? Wait… is he saying?

No…

Ethan Lewis Sullivan is my grandson, son of Elizabeth Marie Sullivan who was daughter to Olivia Hurley-Welling who should have become a Sullivan herself as my fated mate. If you cannot love him the same as before, do him a favor and let him run as he is thinking of doing. Do not subject him to your hatred of my kind. I cannot bear the thought of him hating himself more than he already does.

Let him run away? I stare at this vampire like he's speaking Greek.

Let Ethan go?

NEVER, my wolf growls out. I agree wholeheartedly. Ethan is ours. He's always been ours and always will be ours and no one and nothing will ever change that. His wolf is mine. His heart is mine. His soul is mine. His pain is mine. Everything that makes up my boy is mine and I'll never give him up.

The king levels me with a look of relief.

"I worried your father's influence ran too deep in you," he admits with a sigh. "Your grandfather made a promise, a blood oath, and it was broken. I need the answers for that, but it will have to wait. My grandson needs you more than I need answers. I will be in touch, Alaric."

With that, he speeds away from me. Within seconds, the night is void of the smell of vampires. Their speed is truly frightening.

In the backseat, I slide to the middle so I can hold my boy all the way home. He's so still. I've never seen this side of one of his breakdowns before. I mean we've had our share of them since the summer, but this almost catatonic state is so much worse than the screaming and fighting. It's like my bluebird isn't here. The body in my arms is just an empty shell right now.

Connor and Max both look back in worry multiple times over

the course of the drive home. None of us know what to say. We don't want to trigger something else by accident.

Jack is waiting for us in the garage. When he sees Ethan's face, he frowns and heads inside ahead of us. Max takes him to the kitchen to explain while I head toward the stairs to put Ethan to bed. Connor is talking to Seb and nodding about something. I'll deal with him later. Right now, all that matters is getting my boy to bed and bringing back his smile... somehow.

Opening the door to our room, I am not even paying attention to my surroundings until Ethan jumps out of my arms and races to the bed. This is the first movement he's made on his own since before I put him in the car. He snatches up Mr. Whiskers from the bed and collapses into sobs...

So that was the issue. He went through all of that tonight without Mr. Whiskers.

"I'm sorry. I'm sorry. I'm sorry..." Ethan keeps whispering apologies into the bear's neck as he clings tightly enough that I worry he's going to hurt himself with Stabby.

Why is he apologizing to the bear?

Does it matter? My wolf asks me.

No. It doesn't matter, not right now anyway. I don't even bother to undress before I grab both my boy and his bear in my arms and drag them to the center of the bed. I let him cling to me long after his sobs turn to soft snores.

How in the hell do I help him through this? I'm horribly out of my depth. I just want to make him better. I don't want him to hurt anymore. Goddess, let me take his pain...

7

———

Unburied

Ric

Waking up to an empty bed sets my heart racing, but I calm down once I smell the burnt bacon. My bluebird is trying to cook me breakfast again. He insists he will master the ultimate crispiness of bacon, but it usually just ends up burning. We all choke it down to spare his feelings, but he knows it's not right. Every time, it gets a little better, so he's getting there. Looking at the clock, I see I only managed about three and a half hours of sleep. I'm not usually awake at five in the morning, but it's not unheard of.

After doing my business in the bathroom, I put on fresh jeans and a t-shirt. To make my boy happy, I'm wearing one of the shirts he got me for Christmas. It's the same blue as his eyes and says, "Not the Mama, but close." He recently discovered that old Dinosaur show from the nineties and is *obsessed* with the baby dinosaur. I don't remember the show at all, but then again, I don't even know if I was born yet when it was on.

Walking into the kitchen, I see the disaster zone has mostly been contained to just the stove and the two counters on the sides this time. Thanksgiving was probably the worst. We ended up with pizza that night and for Christmas dinner, we just ordered Chinese. I think next year, I am going to just hire a professional to cater the holiday meals. As for this breakfast, it's probably the cleanest I've ever seen it when Ethan decides to try and cook for us. Then again, it's so early he hasn't really had a chance to make his usual mess yet.

I go to the coffee maker and pop in the pod for the coffee I prefer. Ethan likes the donut shop blends and medium roasts the best. I prefer the dark roasts like French or Columbian. We fought over coffee for the first month or so before this machine suddenly appeared on the counter. I'm pretty sure Connor bought it to stop our bickering… either that or Max picked it up at Jack's suggestion. No matter, it managed to stop our morning grumblings about the coffee.

"Morning, Sweetheart," I tell Ethan, giving him a kiss on the cheek before I take my seat at the counter. The island is for him and Jack. They've both made it abundantly clear that the island is an adult free zone. Never mind the fact that Ethan is technically an adult at twenty-one, he's still a kid to everyone here and is in fact younger than Jack at times… so the island is theirs.

Ethan hasn't answered me. I look up from my tablet to see he's concentrating way too hard on whatever he's trying not to burn at the stove. I don't like my boy being so serious. He's supposed to be all smiles and laughing about how much he still sucks at cooking. It's our thing. He praises my mediocre skills in the kitchen and then I make sure he knows how much I love that he is trying and how much he is improving.

I walk over to the stove and turn off the burners. We don't need breakfast. We need to have a conversation. Last night is apparently still really bothering him, and I can't take it seeing him like this.

Taking him by the hand, I pull him into my arms for a hug. He's so stiff that I'm worried he's going to do something drastic like run away again. Isn't that what the vampire said he wants to do? I can't lose him again. It would kill me for him to choose to stay away from me.

Let's go talk in my office for a bit, ok? I send over to him as I kiss his cheek again.

His nod is jerky and I'm really concerned that something broke inside of him last night that I can't fix. I don't want to go against his wish for no therapy, but I'm out of ideas. He needs a professional or at the very least someone who isn't us to talk to. The love him until he feels safe method isn't working.

Grabbing our coffees, I lead a very solemn Ethan and Mr. Whiskers to my office down the hall. When I turn around after closing the door, I see my boy curled up on one of the chairs in front of my desk, holding Mr. Whiskers like it'll disappear if he relaxes even a millimeter. Something very wrong happened with his panic attack last night and I need to know what it was so that we can prevent that trigger if at all possible.

I'm sorry, Daddy. I'll be better.

Oh, hell no! My boy is not going to be blaming himself for having feelings. I wish I could go back and kill Mr. and Mrs. Sinclair all over again. They did this to him. They made him believe he had no value. He is priceless. He is and always has been deserving of love and affection and they took that from him. They took his heart from him long before he was physically taken away.

"You have nothing to apologize for, Baby," I tell him as I kneel in front of him. I reach up to run my fingers through his hair. I want him to look at me, but he keeps his face buried in Mr. Whiskers' neck. That's alright, though. I want him to be relaxed more than I need the eye contact.

"What happened last night was not your fault. You are allowed to have feelings. You are allowed to express yourself. You are allowed to make mistakes."

Something is going on in his head that I'm not aware of. I'm missing something. Last night's breakdown is not what he's upset about, or at least not fully. There's more to the story and he's holding it inside himself, blaming himself. What the hell happened?

It is all my fault. Everything is my fault. I killed my mother and now I'm going to end up getting you killed too.

Killed his mother? What the hell?

I pull him into my arms. I don't know where this is coming from. I don't know what to do. I need Connor. I need Max. I need someone who can help me figure it out because I'm lost and need a rescue. I'm terrified that if the deal wasn't in effect, I wouldn't have my boy next to me. I can't do this alone.

Ethan

After crying my eyes out last night, I am in desperate need of hydration when I climb out of bed. I sneak down to the kitchen for a bottle of one of the sports drinks. Daddy doesn't like me having that much sugar on an empty stomach, but crying depletes your electrolytes too, right? So I'm just replacing what I lost during my little freak out.

Once I finish my bottle, I decide coffee is in order, so I brew me up my donut shop blend and add a splash of the white chocolate mocha creamer. It's my favorite flavor of the week. Ok, so it just happens to be the one that is open right now. I would change creamers like I change my underwear if I could get away with it. I love almost all of them, except the cheesecake ones. They taste funny and nothing like cheesecake.

Sipping my coffee, I try to remember what all happened last

night. I remember the stuff at school. I remember waking up in the office and grabbing Stabby to defend myself...

Oh yeah, I didn't have Stabby. I lost Mr. Whiskers...

I'm a terrible person. I don't know why they all put up with me. I lost my bestest friend and didn't even notice until I was in danger. I was counting on him, but it was all my fault he wasn't there. I just use him with no regard for his wishes. I'm sure he doesn't want to be stuffed in a backpack all the time. He isn't some dirty secret I'm ashamed of.

I pick him up off of the island and hug him to my chest. *I'll never hide you away, ever again. I'm not ashamed of you. I'll treat you better. I promise... just don't leave me, please? I love you and need you and will never take advantage of you again.*

I know he hears me. I can see it in his beady little eyes. He's forgiven me this time, but I can't let there be a next time. I can't lose him, too. I can't lose any of them. I put them all in danger last night. It was all because of me.

I never should have stuck my nose in the business of other wolves. They aren't even wolves of our pack. The right thing to do would be to contact their Alpha and let him deal with them, but I don't even want to know an Alpha that would let their betas behave that way towards women. I still should have stayed out of it. I just had to play the hero.

Because of me trying to be something I'm not, everyone I love is now in danger. The vampires could have killed all of us on sight for trespassing. The Heartstone pack Alpha can still declare war on us for what I did to his betas. Ric had to... he had to be there because of me...

I made my Daddy hurt again.

I'll make him breakfast to make him smile again. Some bacon and pancakes should be good. Yeah, I'll do that and then he won't be sad and angry anymore. I put everyone in danger. I almost took everyone away from Jackie. It's all my fault. I have to be the one to make everything right again.

I don't even realize Ric has come into the kitchen until I feel the brush of his lips on my cheek. I can't look at him. I can't say anything. If I try, the only thing that will come out will be a sob. I have to be strong. I'm not allowed to break again. I deserve to feel like this. It's my fault. I need to take responsibility for my actions. There are no mistakes without consequences... no second chances... no forgiveness, not for me.

Daddy's turning off the stove. Oh, no. I messed up really bad this time. He's so mad at me. He doesn't even want to eat my food. I mean, I know it's not the greatest, but I was really paying attention this time. I only burned a couple pieces of bacon so far...

I let him pull me to his office. I haven't let go of Mr. Whiskers since I started cooking. Curling up in the chair, I'm ready for Daddy to tell me how much of a disappointment I am. I'm ready for him to blame me, tell me to get out. I clutch Mr. Whiskers like a lifeline, hoping against all odds that Daddy doesn't throw me out like the trash that I am. I deserve it. I deserve everything that's happened.

He goes from stroking my hair to throwing his computer monitor into the wall. This is it. This is the end of my happiness. Why did I ever make that deal? He shouldn't have to be stuck with someone like me. He doesn't deserve this. Goddess, can't you get him a better boy and let me out of this deal? I don't want to do this anymore.

I can't even hear what he's saying. I just want to disappear. I want to go back to my cave. I deserve to be alone forever. All I do is hurt people. They don't deserve to be cursed with me in their lives. I need to leave here. I need to set them free.

Ric storms out of his office, slamming the door behind him. I don't blame him. I'm mad at me too. Uncurling from the chair takes a few minutes. Apparently, I was sitting there long enough to cramp up. Time has no meaning to me right now. I just want to get away.

I want to run, but I made a promise after last time. I promised no more running without talking it out with at least Connie or Ric. Since Ric is pissed at me, I have to talk to Connie. I need to run. I need to get away from everyone. But a promise is a promise and we even did a pinky swear so it's super important to keep it.

Connie? You up? I reach out tentatively. I don't want to wake him up, but I need to talk now.

What's up, little bro? I can hear the yawn in his thoughts. I did wake him up. I'm a terrible person.

I need to run away. I send to him. *All I'm doing is hurting everyone and I need you all to be safe. I made a promise to talk to you, so I'm talking. I'll figure out where to go, but I'm leaving.*

Before he can reply, I cut the link. I'm not sure where we're going, but I hold Mr. Whiskers tighter and climb out the window. It's a bit brisk out, and I wish I grabbed a coat, but we're leaving now. I can always snag one from the lost and found on campus if I have to.

Right now, the only person I could possibly handle seeing is Sully. I want to get some answers from him about why he is right there and alive and well not rotting in that damn basement. How is he so close by and yet I was left in that lab, forced to make the damn deal that I wish every day I could undo...

Climbing the closest tree, I start making my way back towards the Heartstone pack so I can get some stuff from school. Hopefully, the dumbasses from last night haven't yet recovered enough to point fingers at me. Best case scenario is that by the time they blame me, I'm long gone and everyone is safe from the Alpha's retribution.

8

Unburied

<u>Ethan</u>

Sneaking on campus is easier than I expected it to be. I guess I'm so used to not being allowed to go anywhere by myself that sneaking becomes the default. It's hard to get it through my head that I'm allowed to just walk down the street. I'm an adult... most of the time. I don't need a babysitter.

Then again, I needed one last night. The one night I successfully ditch the guard Ric assigned to me is the night I start a war between our pack and not just the vampires, but a neighboring pack as well. My skills would be enviable if they weren't a freaking curse. Only I could ever manage to piss off the two most powerful beings in a three thousand mile radius... in a single night... by saving someone...

I need to put this out of my head and do what I came to do. After a quick stop at the lost and found to claim a coat, hat, and gloves from the bins where everything is just kind of thrown, I borrow a new backpack and notebook and some pens from the campus bookstore while the clerk is busy flirting with a cute faerie. OK, I'll be more honest. I'm stealing again. I can't use the credit card or cell phone, so I left them behind. Ric is going to try to be all noble and bring me back, but I refuse to be the reason he dies or Jack is in danger.

I managed somehow to convince a nice secretary in the administration office to lend me some stamps until I "find my wallet." She reminds me of the grandmas I see on the television. She even gave Mr. Whiskers a pat on the head when she said goodbye to us. She looked at me a bit funny when I asked for the stamps, which I'm sure no one really uses anymore, but I can't send anyone to drop the letters off in person.

Sitting in the coffee shop after my pilfering, I can see everything outside on the quad. Mr. Whiskers is sitting in my lap while I try and write the letters I know I need to send. It's not as easy as it was last time. Last time, I was angry. I was leaving them before they left me again. Last time it was self-preservation. This time...

This time is about saving them. It's about taking responsibility for my own mistakes. There is always the possibility that I won't ever see them ever again. I have to make this right before I can go back...

It took forever to find a mailbox to drop the letters. I ended up just deciding to the student union and give them to the person behind the counter. They can take them for me to give to the postman when he comes to deliver the care packages.

I mean yeah, postal mail is outdated and slow, but sending email would mean alerting them that I'm at school and then they'd be here searching the campus for me within hours... not that I know anyone's email address at this point. I highly doubt Connie is still using Conman96 as his email handle. I don't even remember what server it was on. I just remember that was his username for everything back in high school.

I really hope I can come back here to thank the nice secretary grandma lady someday. It's not often that I see the good side of humanity, and people like her restore my faith. They remind me that it's worth it to try to be a better person. It's worth it to save the world for more than just Jackie.

I know where to start now. Putting the pen to the paper, I pour my soul out in writing...

Dear Daddy...

<hr>

Strolling up to the house of Alpha Heartstone, I'm kind of surprised that there's hardly any security. Like there's a sign in the yard saying they have a security system, but there are no guards. There's no gate. There are no sensors or motion detectors anywhere. I actually make it to the door without any resistance. Hell, I walked across the entire pack without seeing a single warrior. All I saw were betas and humans.

It's a trap! Oh man, that thought starts the stress giggles. All I need is a frog-man looking thing in my head making me giggle uncontrollably when the Alpha opens the door. Hugging Mr. Whiskers to my chest, I try to do some deep breathing to get it under control. Last thing I want to do is make it obvious that I'm not sane to the Alpha I'm here to beg forgiveness from. That thought sobers me enough to be able to stop the giggles.

G Lady? Wanna give me a rare burst of some good luck?

I don't get an answer, not that I expected one. But I square my shoulders and ring the doorbell. After a few moments, the door opens to reveal a woman. She's kind of pretty, but I'm not really a good judge when it comes to females. I mean, I know what looks good objectively but I never know if what I think is what others would think. I'm not wired to see females like that.

"Ummm," I start. I wasn't prepared for this. It was supposed to be the Alpha at the door and then I beg his forgiveness and he yells or puts me in a dungeon or something. I'm not supposed to be talking to anyone else.

"Can I help you?" she asks. She looks like she actually cares. "Are you lost?"

"Yeah, uh..." Man this is hard to get out. "Is the Alpha home? I kinda need to apologize for last night."

There. I said it. I got it out. Now it's up to her to pass it along and then I'll be punished and war will be prevented...

"Oh, dear," she says, interrupting my plans. This doesn't sound good for me. "The Alpha went to meet with the king early this morning before dawn. Apparently, there was some business with a few of our betas stepping out of line. He should be back soon if you'd like to come in for some tea."

She steps aside to invite me in. I am not prepared for this at all. How do I act? What do I do? I've never done the adult tea thing! Is it like a tea party? Is she going to hate me when she finds out what I did? I don't want this nice lady to hate me.

I start backing away from the door shaking my head. I can't hurt this nice lady too. The Alpha is going to be mad at me and he'll take it out on this nice lady for being kind to me. I can't let her be kind to me. I can't stay here.

I miss the step in my rush to back up. I fall off the stoop and scramble back to my feet. Turning to run, I collide with something solid, or I should say someone... Looking up I see the stern face of the man who must be the Alpha. He looks like he's in a terrible mood. I'm just going to make it worse. I have to remember, I deserve this... the others don't.

"Please don't be mad at her. She was just being nice. She doesn't know me. She doesn't know what I did..."

I'm rambling and hugging Mr. Whiskers like he'll be ripped away from me. I deserve any punishment he gives out for me, but I will bust out Stabby if I have to in order to protect the nice lady. I'm not a match for an Alpha, but I'll do some damage if it means the nice lady can get away. I'll make sure she can get away.

"Boy, Look at me," he says to me. I hear something in his voice and my wolf is pushing me to respond. I freaking hate Alpha influence and commands. It's an unfair advantage over the rest of us.

Not command. Not influence. Scent familiar. My wolf is making no sense.

Holding Mr. Whiskers in front of my face I glance up again and meet the eyes of Alpha Heartstone... eyes exactly like my own. What in the actual fuck?

Ric

I had to get out of the office earlier. Ethan was so fragile, it physically hurt to look at him like that. I couldn't control my rage and knew I was scaring him. I had to leave the room, so I escaped to the basement gym to work out my issues. Stepping off the treadmill, I look around before I remember I left my phone up in the office. I have no clue how long I've been down here, but I'm at least calm enough to handle being a rock for my boy to lean on now.

Opening the door to the kitchen, it's like walking into a crisis center. There are people everywhere and everyone is on the phone looking absolutely panicked. My warriors are all looking like someone is about to die, while the tech betas in the room are mostly on the phones or computers, frantically searching for something.

"What is going on?" I ask and everyone freezes and turns to me at once. "Who died?" I don't feel like we've lost anyone.

Jack runs into me, grabbing me tighter than I can remember

him ever clutching me since right after our parents died. I suddenly have a pit in my stomach. He wouldn't normally be this upset over me being out of touch for just a couple of hours. Something has happened and I don't like the mood in here.

Connor races into the room, almost colliding with the marble top of the island. Seeing me standing there, he lets out a breath and runs directly to me to grab me by my shoulders. I'm having a bit of trouble keeping my balance since Jackie isn't letting go of me either.

"Ethan took off again!" he says to me in gasping breaths. "Couldn't... find you... Couldn't... keep up..."

My Beta is swaying on his feet and Bastien grabs him under the arms before he crumbles to the ground. Just how long was I down in the gym???

Seb and Bastien start filling me in on what's going on while Connor is out cold. He apparently worked himself past the point of exhaustion. From what they can tell me, after I left the office, Ethan reached out to Connor and told him he's running and apparently something about preventing war? By the time Connor got to the office, Ethan was already out the window and his scent disappeared in the trees as per usual.

He's supposedly shared the secret with Max because of the liability issue, but swore him to secrecy. I'm so lost on what in the hell my boy was thinking. Not only can't any of us follow him, but now he's trying to prevent a war? What war does he think is going to happen? He was kidnapped...

***

While I've been in the gym, everyone has been looking for both of us, and since apparently neither of us have our phones, they were all freaking out. I'm touched that my people were worried about me, but I'm more concerned about Ethan right now. He ran out of the house without a coat. Yeah, it's not below freezing right now, but it's still cold enough to warrant some winter gear. This isn't Florida.

Looking at Seb, I can tell there has been zero news on Ethan so far. Bastian hands over my phone. I can see Ethan's lying on the counter. I know my boy can reach out to any of us if he needs help, but it's not right with me that he doesn't have it considering what I know now. I don't understand why he ran again. It's just not adding up in my head at all.

Scrolling through the missed calls, I see a few from numbers I don't have saved in my phone. I'll check them out in my office. I start moving that way when my phone starts ringing again. It's one of the unknown numbers, so I answer it while I continue walking that way. The rest of the people in the kitchen don't need to know anything just yet and I need to get some space to think.

"Alaric Jameson," I answer. I don't ever reveal myself as Alpha when I answer an unknown call. You never know if the person on the other end is human or if they know about us.

"Good to catch you before I get to bed, Alpha."

It's the vampire. Ethan mentioned stopping a war, does that mean he ran off to the vampires this morning? Did he really think that his grandfather would start a war over that little skirmish last night? My boy really thought himself into a circle with that one... then again, does Ethan know Edward is his grandfather?

"King Edward," I say into the phone and the room goes silent behind me. "Has Ethan arrived there yet? He ran out of here this morning and has everyone quite worried."

There's a weight to the silence on the other end of the line before the call disconnects. I stare at the screen in confusion before I save the contact information for future reference. Scrolling back through the call log, I can see most of the missed calls were from him and only those from the last hour or so have been from the other unknown number.

What do you mean my grandson ran out?

I can hear the vampire in my head. His thoughts, voice, mind, whatever is much clearer than Ethan's even when we're in the same room.

It comes with age and power. Now tell me! Where is my grandson? What the fuck did you do?

Well I'm obviously not his favorite person right now. I enter my office and lock the door so I'm not disturbed while having this conversation. I usually am fine doing this mind speaking with Ethan, but it's weird doing this with someone else. It's difficult to have a conversation inside your mind without accidently speaking aloud.

He had been... off, let's say... since his episode last night. I tell Edward. *He cried himself to sleep and I planned on talking it over with him this morning. When I got up, he was burning breakfast, but that's typical when he tries to cook. When he didn't respond verbally to my greeting, I got worried and brought him to my office. He apologized to me for gods only know what and I got upset.*

At this point, the vampire interrupts me with a growl that even makes my wolf cower a bit. That's not good.

Why the fuck did you get mad at him for apologizing?! He's done nothing wrong! He has zero fault in anything that has been done to him and you are a fucking ass who doesn't deserve him for making him feel even a single speck of blame for that!

I have to interrupt to correct his misconception before this turns to the very war Ethan had been thinking he's causing.

I will never be mad at my mate. I send to him to stop his rant before he really takes off. I understand now where Ethan gets the anger issues. Seeing as how I know my mate, I don't want to ever offend his grandfather. I don't think I'd survive.

I was angry at the situation. I was angry that things keep happening to him. I was angry that I failed yet again to protect him. I was angry at his fucking family, Connor excluded, who raised him to believe that he is worthless and always to blame and deserving of being punished even when he's done nothing wrong. I was angry at the damn Sinclairs for fucking destroying his childhood to the point he doesn't know how to accept even basic affection without thinking he has to earn it.

I don't even know if the vampire is still listening. My rage, which was banked after my time in the gym, has come back to the surface. I wish there was another person out there to blame for Ethan's treatment that I could work my frustration out on, but we took care of them all. There's no one left unless there are more from the lab that we don't know about yet... and my boy doesn't talk about the lab. He doesn't talk about any of it.

I lay my head on the cool desk, hoping to calm the storm in my heart. I know he's alive. I know he's not injured... at least physically. My boy is tearing himself apart on the inside though, blaming himself, for other people's actions because that's all he's ever known. When is he going to realize that he is blameless in all of this? When is my bluebird going to realize that our love is without strings or conditions?

10

Unburied

Ric

John and Esther neglected him?

So the asshole is still there, huh. Well I guess it's time to give him a bit of a back story in case Ethan does make an appearance there.

Yeah, neglect. That's a nice way to put it...

Esther started experimenting on him when he was four years old. She had a lab in the basement that she would tie him up in, cut him open, beat him until all of his bones were broken, suffocated him, and brought him to the brink of death over and over and over again for eight years. John knew what was going on and did nothing to stop his wife. Connor and I were clueless. Ethan told no one... Apparently, my dad knew some of it, but I don't know how much.

I can feel the tension through our connection. Edward is seeking out a specific answer that I haven't exposed yet. He's not worthy of my deepest shame, but I know that is what he wants. He wants to know how in the hell it was possible for a pup to be abused like this in a respectable pack like ours. He wants to know why it was never brought to his attention. I can feel it.

Edward is not worthy of knowing our pack secrets, the shame...

*But mate is...*says our wolf. Damnit he's right. I'll do anything for Ethan, even bare my soul to the enemy.

I'm not your enemy Edward sends to me. I can't trust that just yet, but I almost want to. He loves Ethan. His willingness to let us all leave last night and not demand compensation for the damages proved that.

Can we continue this later? I just want to find my boy first, I send back to him. I can't waste any more time. I need to start my search.

I will come to your lands at sundown. Make sure I don't have to kill your warriors when I arrive. He sends to me before I feel the connection sever.

A vampire on my lands... my world has just gone complete topsy turvy and the only thing I want to happen is for my boy to reach out to me to come back home. I want to go out to the living room and see that he and Jack have converted the entire room back into their pillow fort... I can't believe there are that many pillows in this house, but the boys grabbed all of them. I'd never seen Jack so happy as he was that day...

I must have dozed for a bit at my desk because I wake up to my phone ringing next to my head and realize there's a paper stuck to my face as I sit up. I don't even look at the screen before I answer. I'm not exactly the most coherent when I first wake up.

"What?" I growl into the phone. The call disconnects. I rip the paper away from my face and what I just did registers in my brain. In a panic, I look at the screen and see it's the other number that had been calling this morning. Oh shit. What if that was my boy and I just proved to him I'm angry. I feel fear that isn't my own before it cuts off. I almost hear a sob. Oh gods, it *was* him...

Ethan? Baby? You can talk to me. I'm sorry I growled. I'm not mad at you. Please, Blue. Just come home to us.

It's like talking to a brick wall. I don't know if he is hearing me and not responding or if he's completely blocked himself off. Either way, I have to get him to talk to me. Picking up the phone again, I call the number back that just called me.

It rings through to voicemail. The question of who the number belongs to is answered, but why the fuck is Ethan with him?

"You have reached the voicemail of Bennet Heartstone. Leave me a message and I will return your call. If this is an emergency for the business, please hang up and send a text."

After the beep, I leave a rushed message, "Alpha Heartstone, this is Alpha Jameson. Please have my mate reach back out to me as soon as possible. Tell him I fucked up. Tell him I'm sorry. Please just tell him."

I disconnect and wait. Every second feels like an eternity before the phone rings again. It could have been minutes or hours. It's all the same without my boy here. The ringing almost makes me fall from my seat and I hurry to answer the call after seeing that it's Alpha Heartstone's number.

"Ethan?" I ask as soon as I pick up the phone.

"No," growls the voice on the other end. "Your mate has requested sanctuary in my pack and I have granted it. I don't know what the fuck you learned from your father, Jameson, but in my pack, we respect and treat our mates with kindness and love. We don't abandon them and drive them out. You're a selfish and narcissistic pup just like your old man and until Ethan says he wants to go back to you, you will not see him ever again."

I'm still in shock as the phone disconnects. Ethan requested sanctuary? My mate has officially left me and I can't go get him. I can't even set foot on Heartstone land without it being a declaration of war. What the fuck have I done?

11

Unburied

Bennet Heartstone

This is not what I was expecting leaving King Edward's house. Had fate worked out the way it should have, he would have been my father-in-law, but unfortunately greed and prejudice took my mate away from me before I was able to truly get to know her. Those few weeks were the best of my life, and my wolf has never recovered. Lisa tries her best, but she will never be Elizabeth. My heart will always belong to my Lizzie.

I never told Edward that his daughter was my mate. The day he killed my father and put me in place as Alpha of the pack, I saw in his eyes the same sorrow I witnessed in my Lizzie's eyes. She had his eyes. He lost her just the same as me. I never knew how she died. I couldn't ever bring myself to ask him.

The Jameson pack had a change in leadership before ours did and the new Alpha was cagey as all hell. Then when he moved his pack next door to mine, I really wondered what his deal was. He mentioned something about a tragedy and his Beta's family being in an accident. I didn't really buy that since the only ones I saw showing any signs of grief were his own son and the young Beta. Two grieving wolves doesn't necessitate relocating an entire pack. The man was running from something, but I could never figure out what.

I kept an eye on him for a couple years, not trusting him in the slightest. He was constantly upping his security. He acted like an attack was imminent on his pack. Apparently, he knew something was catching up to him because he panicked and ran again, this time with just his wife and a single warrior. His car ended up going off a cliff as he was trying to run. Rumor has it, he left his twenty-one-year-old son with his toddler son to raise. The bastard abandoned both of his kids.

I'm angry enough without dragging up the past. I'm better off thinking back on the ungodly early meeting with King Edward. Apparently, some of the idiot beta college kids decided to make asses of themselves. Edward called me to come pick them up and explain the situation, so that I wouldn't take revenge on his grandson...

Like I would ever punish someone for defending themselves.

But yeah, the boy did an awful lot of damage for not delivering a single killing blow. It also looks like he used silver so the wounds will heal human slow and might even scar those idiots. Is it wrong to say I'm proud of him? I mean, any dumbass with a blade can kill. There are so many places to cut and slice open that will result in death before the healing will kick in. It's so easy to do it by accident, especially with silver. My head warrior has screwed up with that a time or two. But this kid, this omega wolf, managed to do it not once, but three times.

All three boys will live, unfortunately. I can't really punish them further since the victim already gave a harsher punishment than I would ever have given out for the same crime. Maybe I should change my way of doing things? If these betas think that their behavior on campus is acceptable, there probably should be harsher punishments.

OK thoughts are getting away from me again. I wish ADHD meds would work with our metabolisms. There are times when my brain is a truly frightening situation of a dozen squirrels running in twenty seven directions while I'm trying to focus. It's not a good thing when you're trying to run a pack.

I pull into the driveway still reeling over the fact that I never knew my Lizzie had a kid and wondering who the father could have been. She wasn't supposed to be able to be pregnant. Hybrids with humans aren't supposed to be fertile and we thought she was human hybrid. We were both under the age of full maturity. She was only fifteen to my seventeen. Hell, I wasn't even fully certain she was my mate. There was no way to find out after she died.

From the way Edward was talking about him, I guessed this Ethan was barely eighteen. I mean, what twenty-one-year-old is taking intro level classes?

As I get out in the driveway and head across the lawn, my attention is drawn to the front stoop where I see Lisa inviting a strange wolf into our house. Before I can even react, the boy backs away from her in a panic, falling off the stoop in his rush to leave. I guess he doesn't see me, because he smacks face first into my chest.

He glances at my face before bowing his head and starts apologizing and saying not to hurt Lisa. Why does this kid think I'm going to hurt my chosen mate? Who hurt this kid so much that he's this anxious?

I tell him to look at me so that I can reassure him, but when our eyes meet, I see my own eyes reflected back. He has Lizzie's looks, but those are my eyes and my red hair. The boy on my lawn is my own son that I just found out about. Apparently, he sees it too because he faints dead away, right there on my lawn... not exactly the first impression I wanted to make on my Lizzie's boy... well, my boy, I guess.

Lisa is frantic as I carry him into the house and put him in one of the guest rooms upstairs. I don't exactly have a reputation for being kind to strangers, but I will always offer assistance to those who truly need it. After, tucking him in, I turn to see my mate in the doorway with a soft smile on her face.

"He's yours, isn't he?" she asks me holding her middle. She tried so desperately to have a child with me. We both knew we weren't fated, but we still hoped the Goddess would grant us a babe. She didn't answer our prayers... but now she has returned my son to me. This must be killing my mate to see the proof of fate's blessing lying in the bed while her womb has remained barren.

I nod and lead Lisa back down to the lounge where she had set up for her tea time. She always has morning tea around ten or so. She has her tea and we do brunch or if I'm running late, we'll do a late lunch. It's become our routine. But today, we need to change things up.

We have a nice long discussion regarding my time with Lizzie and all the years of not knowing. I even tell her of the complicated relationship I have with King Edward. She had always assumed the tension I felt toward him was due to my father's death. I let her believe that for years, but now I reveal the truth.

He was Lizzie's father and I was the bastard who was supposed to be with her. I couldn't even commiserate with him or share our grief because there had been no way of truly knowing she was my fated mate. I explain to Lisa that I didn't know Lizzie had a child until this morning and that I wasn't aware that child was mine until I saw him.

She just sighs and leaves the room. My eyes follow her while my heart is breaking for her. She wanted a child so badly, and here I had one just dropped right in my life with no connection to her. My sorrow morphs to surprise when I see her come back into the house carrying a ratty old teddy bear up the stairs. The boy must have dropped it outside when he fainted. I didn't even notice, but she did. I might not love her like I loved Lizzie, but Lisa has her own place securely in my heart.

Edward told me the boy is mated to the Alpha of the Jameson pack. I don't have much faith in the kid to be better than his father. Just like I expected, the phone is going unanswered as I try to get in touch with him. I refuse to leave a voicemail regarding such an important matter, so I just try to call a few more times over the course of the next couple of hours.

What kind of man doesn't answer the phone when his mate is missing?

My son wakes up from his impromptu nap and makes his way down the stairs just after one. Lisa is in the kitchen making some lunch for us all, so I invite the boy into the dining room for a chat. He looks thoroughly subdued, as if all the light in the world can't touch him. What the hell happened to my son? What the hell is going on in that damn pack that my son had to run away?

Ethan spends the next hour explaining what happened last night with my betas and that he really didn't want anything to do with them and that I shouldn't blame his "Daddy" or his brother or any of the Jameson pack for what he did. He actually thought I would go to war over what he did to the idiots who deserved every cut.

It takes every ounce of willpower to hold back my rage and tears while Ethan tells me and Lisa what happened. This boy has decided to take all the blame on himself and even surrendered to a potential enemy just to make sure the ones he loves will be safe. He has his mother's heart. Gods know, I am a selfish bastard, so he didn't get that from me.

When he asks to use my phone, I don't hesitate. He wants to let his Daddy know he is alright and that everything has worked out. Nothing against anyone in that kind of relationship, but I can feel my wolf get a bit on edge every time I hear him say Daddy in reference to his Alpha. Was that what the little prick told him he had to call him? Or is it a consensual thing that my son is truly into? I really need to hear that my son isn't being forced in any way, but I can't believe that when I witness their interaction on the phone.

The call connects, but all I hear is a growl and a shout and Ethan hurriedly disconnects the call. He starts crying and rocking in his chair, clutching his teddy to his chest. That piece of shit just yelled at his mate? My phone starts ringing, but I hit ignore. I can see that it's him calling back, but my son has completely fallen apart again. Lisa pulls him to her chest before taking him by the arm and leading him back upstairs to the bedroom.

I wait until I can hear her singing him a lullaby before I grab the phone and head to my office where it is soundproof. Then I call the asshole back and inform him of exactly where he stands with me and essentially declare war if he tries to force Ethan to go back to him.

My son will be safe with me. My son will not be treated the way his mother was. My son can live without his mate just like I did. I won't let the Jameson pack ruin another person I love.

12

Ethan

Waking up in this bed again is a very strange sensation. I miss waking up to Daddy being next to me, but he was so mad before. I just wanted to tell him I fixed everything and he growled at me. I always knew he would get sick of me eventually, but I didn't think it would be so soon. I was hoping to at least get to experience all the coupley things with him first. We didn't even make it to Valentine's Day... and I ordered him such an awesome gift...

At least he'll have that to remember me by. I hope he doesn't throw it out. It was a lot of money. He should at least try to return it if he doesn't want it. I'll try to get the suggestion to him through Connor or Max since he doesn't want to talk to me anymore...but seeing as how neither of them have said anything or reached out, I don't know if they do either.

Anyways, it's my fault for trying to call him in the first place. I knew he was already mad and instead of waiting for him to get the letter, I got excited that I fixed it for him. I thought I was doing what I should since it was my mess and all. Was I wrong? I just don't know what I'm doing here.

For so many years of my life, I had only one goal... survive to get to my mate and he would make everything better. He was supposed to save me. He was supposed to fix me... He was supposed to protect me. He was supposed to *want* me...

Last month, I had my heat again. I thought the claiming bite was supposed to stop my heats, but no. All it does is make it so that only Ric can smell my pheromones. I still lose my mind and want to fuck for three days straight, but the only one who wants to fuck me is Ric... supposedly. He wasn't there when it started and he wasn't there when I came out of it. I don't blame him. Who wants a broken omega?

And I am broken. I'm like a toy that was dropped and the pieces aren't all there anymore. It kinda looks alright from far away, but you can't touch it or it will just fall apart. You can use glue, but then it only looks good and serves no other purpose. I'm not ok with just looking the part. I want to be whole again. I want to be loved again. I want my Daddy back, but he doesn't want me anymore.

There's a knock on the door, so I quickly wipe the tears away and sit up. Here's the nice lady again. I think she said her name is Lisa, but I can't remember. She looks like she should be someone's mom. She was nice and sang to me to help me sleep earlier. No one has ever done that for me. I thought lullabies were just a myth before today.

"Why aren't you a mom?" I ask out loud. I didn't mean to do that, especially with seeing her flinch. I know what it's like to not be able to have a baby. Granted our situations are likely very different.

"The Goddess has not seen fit to make me a mother," she tells me with a soft smile. There's something behind her look. Does she know that the Alpha is my bio dad? I mean I'm pretty sure he's my sperm donor, but he could be an uncle or someone in the same family though. I haven't confirmed it.

"You should come down for dinner," she continues. "I just pulled the meatloaf out of the oven and it should be ready to eat by the time you come down."

Meatloaf? I've heard of it, but never tried it. Mom... *Mrs. Sinclair...* refused to consume anything that could be remotely considered delicious aka high in fat or triglycerides or whatever. It wouldn't have killed her to use spices. But then again, maybe she did cook the good stuff and just never let me have any. Connie never complained.

Lisa chuckles at my obvious excitement and heads back down the stairs. I'm going to get to try meatloaf. Ooooh! Meatloaf usually goes with mashed potatoes, right? I think that's what they always show on TV. I love mashed potatoes! Now, I'm really excited for dinner...

I jump out of the bed and hear a thump. Looking down, I see Mr. Whiskers on the floor. I almost forgot him again! Oh, no. I can't forget him. The Alpha and Lisa didn't seem to mind me holding him before when we were talking, but are they going to make a big deal about him being at the table?

I hope not. I really want to try meatloaf. I mean I REALLY want to try it. But if Mr. Whiskers isn't welcome at the table, then neither am I. He is NEVER being left behind again.

I hurry through my bathroom routine and make sure both Mr. Whiskers and I wash our hands. It's important to be hygienic before meals. Once I'm certain we're both as presentable as we can be, I carry him down and into the dining room...

There are four places set at the table...

I'm so not up for dealing with company, and I look over at the Alpha in panic.

"I'm not really that hungry, so I'm going to go back upstairs," I rush out as I turn to run for the stairs.

He stands up and blocks my way, grabbing onto my shoulders and forcing me to stop. I look up at him and he's smiling down at me. I've never had a grown up look at me like this before. Is this how they looked at Connie? Is that why he's so amazing? There's a happy butterfly feeling in my tummy, not the icky kind. I want this man to be my father. Oh, please universe, let him be my dad.

I can't stop the tears and he pulls me into his chest. This is what I've wanted my whole life. I just want someone to hold me. I don't need pretty lies. I don't need to put on a show. I just need to be held and wanted and... I can't fall apart here. These people are strangers... But I want to trust them...

Alpha Heartstone holds me as I let everything out that has built up over the last two days, and honestly the last twenty-one years of parental abandonment. I don't even know if he knows I'm his kid, I hope I am anyways. He's a good dad. He should have a kid. Him and Lisa should have a kid. He shouldn't be stuck with a screw up like me.

"Enough of that," he says to me while running his fingers through my hair. "Yes, you are my son and Elizabeth was my fated mate. You are what we have left of her, and that is enough."

So he loves my mom and not me? Well that just shattered all the hopes I had that I finally found someone who will love me for me. No one wants me for me. I'm Ric's mate. I'm Elizabeth's son. I'm Connor's brother. I'm the Goddess's plaything...

"You are my son and I love you for you," Bennet says to me, lifting my chin to force eye contact. "We are going to talk about this more in depth after dinner, but little tummies need to eat so we all have the strength to talk about the hard stuff."

Did he say little tummies?

I can't stop the giggle that comes out. Just how much did he figure out about me already?

Lisa comes in the room to interrupt the very confusing father son moment that is going on. As she places the food on the table, she indicates one of the settings as mine, so I sit with Mr. Whiskers in my lap. Bennet takes the seat to my left at the head of the table and Lisa takes the seat across from me.

"Are we waiting on someone else?" I ask them. It's rude to start before everyone is there. I learned that lesson very early on in the Sinclair house... and I was never allowed to be rude when it came to guests...or in front of grownups in general.

Bennet chuckles and Lisa gets back up and grabs a pile of books off of the side table in the lounge. She places them on the chair and returns to her seat. At my look of confusion, she explains, "The seat is for your teddy if he wants it. I forgot the books so that he can see over the table."

OK this lady is my new Mom. No ifs, ands, or buts... Lisa is now Mom. I'm still on the fence with Bennet. After all, he did knock up my mom and ditch her as a teenager, so he can't be as noble and shit as he appears to be.

"Alright, Ethan," Bennet starts and I look up at him to see what he has to say. Lisa is cutting the meatloaf and the smell is super distracting. I want to pay attention, I really do... but oh my goddess, this smell is divine...

"Kid, hasn't anyone ever told you that you need to learn to block your thoughts?" Bennet manages to get out between chuckles.

Oh, shit... I'm broadcasting again? I really have to work on this. I swear I have more control over it, but it must just be all of the stress making me forget or something.

"Sorry," I tell them as I fold my hands in my lap and look down. This is it. This is the moment I get the good stuff taken away from me and I have to go to my room. I just wanted to try the meatloaf so badly that I forgot to keep a lock on my thoughts. They're going to send me away too and I have nowhere left to go. The cave isn't even safe anymore since Ric and Max found it last time.

Bennet's growl cuts through my thoughts and makes me look up at him.

"I'm not sending you away. You aren't going anywhere unless you want to... and not because you think we don't want you here," he says as he gets up to come and kneel next to my seat.

Taking my hand in both of his, he continues, "You will never be in trouble for wanting to eat Lisa's delicious cooking." He gives a little wink at that and when I look over at Lisa, she's blushing.

"I don't know what you were taught or what you went through, but in this house you are allowed to think, feel, and express whatever you want to."

When he stands, he kisses me on the forehead before returning to his seat. I feel like I'm in a dream world that I created from one of the shows I see on TV. I always thought those shows were super unrealistic. Now, I'm starting to think my life was the abnormality.

I don't even realize I've taken a bite of the food until the taste registers to my brain. I look at Lisa and see her beaming smile directed at me. OK, if this is what I've been missing, I want more of this in my life.

It vaguely registers that my father is laughing at me while I shovel the food in my face, but I am beyond caring at this point. This is the best thing I've ever tasted. It even beats out fries with chocolate ice cream. I think I'm going to get a tummy ache tonight, but it's so worth it.

13

Unburied

After a tense dinner, I sent Jackie off to his friend's house to spend the night. He fought with me about it because he wants to be home when Ethan comes back. I don't know how to tell him Ethan might not decide to come back home. I screwed up royally this time and totally deserve it if my boy leaves me for good.

Jack arguing with me wasn't helping, so the decision to send him to his friend's house for the night made sense. I don't need to blow up at him as well. The original plan was to have Max take him to a movie for while the vampire is here, but an overnight stay out of the house is safer. The vampire might be Ethan's grandfather, but he's still a bloodsucker...

I want to get over the prejudices that were built up in me. I don't want to look at my boy any differently... and I'm pretty sure I don't. He can't choose who his grandfather is. He has no say in the blood that runs through his veins. But every time I smell a vampire, I have to fight against my revulsion. I can't let my boy see that anymore.

Now, I'm sitting on the front stoop waiting for the sun to go down. I don't know how much information Edward is going to have regarding where Ethan is right now, but I'm hesitant to share what I know. I get the feeling he won't deal with me at all if he finds out his grandson is in another pack seeking sanctuary. Hell, if he wants to, he can wipe our pack out of existence with zero repercussions. The only thing I need out of this meeting is a guarantee that Jack and the other children will be safe no matter what. All of us adults failed Ethan. The kids are innocent.

"I would never harm a child."

I damn near fall off the stoop into the bushes at his spoken words. I didn't even notice he had arrived.

"If you intend to be with my grandson, you had better learn to block your thoughts," he tells me before walking past me into my house. Well, I guess this disproves the whole needing an invitation thing...

"That is just common courtesy, but I'm not going to give that to you at this moment," he says after draping himself in the recliner in the living room. "Now what the fuck did you do to my grandson and where has he gone that you don't want me to know?"

I take a deep breath and sit on the couch while I relay the events of the phone calls early this afternoon. At the revelation that Alpha Heartstone has taken Ethan in and claimed sanctuary for him, Edward's face turns very dark. I don't know if I want to know what that is about. I thought they had a tight alliance, but maybe not?

"And you are sure it is Bennet Heartstone to whom you spoke?"

The vampire is being overly formal this evening. I don't know if that's a good thing or a bad thing in the overall perspective of the situation, but I know it's bad for the relationship with my mate if his family hates me.

"I'm certain. The phone rang to voicemail first and when I got a return call, it was the same voice," I tell him, making sure not to allow any inflection in my voice. I don't know how Edward feels about this bit of information, so I don't want to risk alienating the only ally I possibly have to being able to contact my mate.

"I will have a discussion with Bennet," he says standing up and walking to the front door. Before I can say anything more, he is gone into the night and I see a startled Max at the end of the walkway, coming back from dropping off Jack.

"Did I imagine things or did a vampire just zoom out of here?" he asks as he comes inside, closing the door behind him.

"Not your imagination," I tell him and lead him to my office. Grabbing a bottle of water from my mini fridge, I offer it to him. He walks over and snags a can of soda out of the door instead.

After about five minutes of silence, I break and tell Max everything. I need someone to confide in that isn't going to judge me for losing my temper this morning. I need someone to listen and tell me what I need to hear and not just go off about how I screwed up with my boy over the last twenty-four hours.

"Dude, you fucked up," Max says when I finish with Edward's last words.

At my look, he just shrugs. "You don't come to me for platitudes," he tells me. "This is how I see it... I wasn't here last night beyond dropping you guys off at home. Little dude was in a bad spot, but you all seemed to have it under control. I made sure he had Mr. Whiskers and then I dipped out because... well, I have my reasons..."

He looks a bit disturbed but shakes it off to continue.

"As for this morning, I know I wasn't around... again for reasons. But from what I understand, Ethan still wasn't fully alright after last night. He did what he always does and tried to power through it. You were on the right track for stopping him from cooking, but you didn't listen to what he was saying... or rather not saying."

I'm confused by what Max is talking about. I heard every word that Ethan spoke and sent out this morning.

"What was he blaming himself for so much that I felt the need to apologize? Did you ever ask?" Max is getting agitated as he goes on, "No. Of course you didn't. You just assumed and got angry at the fact that he was yet again apologizing for something that wasn't his fault. You got angry at the situation, but to him you were angry at him. *He* screwed up again..."

Is that really what Ethan was thinking this morning? Does he think I was angry AT him? WITH him? Oh, no. And then I growled on the phone...

My head is in my hands, elbows on the desk. I really fucked up. Max gets up from his chair and heads over to the window. It's much nicer than the one we had to replace last summer. He looks wrung out, which I must be imagining because nothing ever gets to Max like this.

"From what you told me of his conversation with Conner, and who knows how much he actually remembered since the dumbass was still half asleep when Ethan popped into his head, he thinks what he did last night was going to start a freaking war... and so he went off to stop any of us from getting hurt on his behalf." Max levels me with a stare to drive home the point. My boy seriously thinks last night is all his fault and that there are dire consequences as a result.

"Has Heartstone said anything about recompense for his betas?" Max asks me, breaking into my thoughts. I guess he's done giving me the insight into my boy. The cracks in his surface seem to have been just my imagination because he's all business right now.

"No," I tell him. "He actually has taken Ethan in under sanctuary and I can't set foot in their territory unless I'm invited by Ethan himself, or I risk the war that my boy was adamant to prevent in the first place."

The eyes of my warrior are hard as granite and dark as the pits of hell when he asks, "Does that order only apply to you? Or will anyone from this pack incite a war?"

It takes a minute to understand what he's asking. If it applies to everyone, that means the college kids can't attend classes and the adults with jobs at and around the university won't be able to go to work tomorrow. I pick up my phone to call the Alpha to ask, as it affects my whole pack and just not my relationship with my mate.

Max is staring at me like he wants to hurt me. Yeah, I'm a shitty Alpha for not thinking of this sooner... My personal life is always going to affect my pack, but it should never put their livelihoods or futures in jeopardy like this.

I put the phone on speaker and place it on the table. We listen as it rings through to voicemail. I hang up and try again. I cannot afford to wait for him to return my call or risk him not even listening... Voicemail again.

At this point, Max snatches up my phone and copies the number into his own. He throws my phone back at me and calls Alpha Heartstone himself. He doesn't put it on speaker, but holds it to his ear, glaring at me the entire time.

I understand the anger at the position I've put him in as my head warrior. He's responsible for the safety and security of the whole pack and I managed to make his life so much more complicated because I didn't stop to ask my boy a question.

"Is this Alpha Heartstone?" he asks, breaking a bit of the tension that has built up between us. Apparently his call was answered. I can't hear anything on the other end of the conversation. Max must have his volume set extremely low, and I'm a bit hurt that he's not allowing me to hear.

"Yes, he's here but he's not a part of this conversation if you don't want him to be."

What? He's giving another Alpha preferential treatment? My wolf starts grumbling, but I hold him back so that we can try to get an answer on our boy and the future treatment of the pack. I watch Max as he paces the floor of my office and talks with another Alpha on behalf of my pack because I can't. I don't like this helplessness.

"My name is Max... Head warrior... You can ask Ethan about me, but I need to clarify the stipulations of the sanctuary.... Uh huh... yes... does it apply to only Ric or to the rest of the pack? Oh... ok... the university only, then? Alright. Yes. Understood. Tell the little dude he can call me for anything, ok? Thank you Alpha... Bennet then... Thank you... And you as well."

As he puts his phone back in his pocket, Max heads straight towards the door. He's never been this cold and shut off to me before. It's like the phone call, or the last twenty four hours changed something in our dynamic. I don't understand what is going on.

He's zipping up his coat as he tells me, "Our pack can go to the university and their jobs within his territory, but only if they are scheduled to be there. No college visits are allowed unless previously scheduled and absolutely no warriors or anyone near any of the homes in the territory."

"Where are you going?" I ask him. This is too business like for him. I don't ever remember a time when Max wasn't at least a little bit of a smartass, but his eyes have no spark in them now.

"I'll pick Jack up and bring him home when you're ready for

him to come home, Alpha," he says as he bows his head to me. "I'm going to go take care of some things... personal things."

And with that, he leaves me standing in my front hallway, staring at the closed door. I went from having a house full of laughter and people to being alone in the empty and silent house. What the fuck just happened?

Ethan

After dinner, I help Bennet with the cleanup in the kitchen. I think it's pretty cool that even though he's the Alpha, he still does dishes so his mate can relax after cooking. Maybe I should start doing the dishes for Ric since he cooks most of the time?

We all jump at the crash of the tumbler shattering against the tile floor. I didn't mean to do it! I just got lost in my thoughts and it slipped. I didn't mean it!

I crouch down and start picking up the pieces as quickly as possible so that there is not a mess. There can't be a mess. I am in so much trouble now. They are going to have to buy a whole new set because I messed it all up now and people will talk about how the set doesn't match now and I'll get the looks every time they have to pull out a glass and...

Lisa is pulling me into a hug from behind and Bennet has a broom and dustpan to sweep up the glass. She gently pries my fist open so that the glass I had already picked up can be added to the dustpan and leads me to the sink so that she can start to clean my wound.

What is going on? I'm so confused. Why aren't they yelling? Why did they clean up my mess? I'm supposed to clean it up. I clean up all the messes on the floor. They're always my fault.

Why is she helping me? Maybe she just doesn't want the blood all over the place... that sounds right. But why is she holding me and talking softly. She should be yelling. Why aren't they yelling at me?

I'm completely numb as I'm led to the sofa in the lounge. Lisa sits on one side of me, keeping me tucked in her arms and humming that song she was singing earlier. I like this song. It makes me want to smile, but I shouldn't smile. I made a mess and they cleaned it...

Bennet comes into the room from the other direction. I didn't notice him cutting through, but then again I haven't really seen much of the house just yet. Maybe there's a secret hallway or something. He's not alone, though and the super old vampire dude is with him. I don't remember his name, but I know he's really really old.

The realization hits me and I try to push away from Lisa. Oh, no... I'm in trouble still. I stopped the war with the wolves with Bennet being my bio dad and all but I forgot about the vamps. They're going to wipe out my whole family and it's all my fault. I try to get away, but Lisa isn't letting me go. I never should have stayed here...

"Bio dad?!" the vampire dude yells at Bennet, picking him up by his throat and dangling him like he weighs nothing more than Mr. Whiskers.

The vampire dude looks really fucking mad and it's all my fault. I just found out who my dad is and got to experience what it would be like to have real parents for only a few hours...of course, I screwed it up. Now, Lisa is going to lose her mate and she won't want me around and I'll lose her too and it's all my fault...

I stop trying to get away and just collapse in on myself. I ruin everything and everyone around me. I caused enough death. I killed my mother. I don't want my father to die because of me, too.

Bennet is dropped to the ground before he went from the red face stage of suffocation to the purple stage, so I know he's going to be alright. Before the vampire can attack him again, I step in the way.

Stay the fuck away from him! I send out as forcefully as I can. *He's done nothing more than take me in and give me a meal. Your problem is with me, not them!*

The vamp dude looks at me in surprise, followed by sadness.

"I'm not angry at you, Ethan. You have no control over who your sperm donor was..." he starts glaring at Bennet laying on the ground next to the coffee table. "Bennet is the one who had sex with a fifteen year old and impregnated her and abandoned her!"

"I was a kid, too!" Bennet yells back at him, trying to get to his feet. "I was seventeen... and she was the most wonderful person I had ever met! She must have gotten it from her mother because I sure as hell never saw it in you."

Wait... what?

Lisa seems to catch on quick and grabs my hand to pull me back to the sofa before my legs give out on me. My brain isn't math-ing correctly, right?

Bennet is bio dad.

Elizabeth is bio mom.

Elizabeth's mom is Uncle Carl and fake mom's mom.

Elizabeth's dad is... vampire dude???

The vampire hangs his head and chuckles out, "My name is Edward, not vampire dude. And yes, you are "math-ing" correctly. I am your maternal grandfather."

I lean back into the sofa in a daze. Huh... so that means I'm part vampire... I'm part the thing that Ric hates most in the world. I'm part thing that everyone hates. They were right to try to destroy me. I'm an abomination... just like they always said... I shouldn't exist...

Lisa hands me Mr. Whiskers and I clutch him to my chest. I can only count on him. He's the only one who doesn't care what I am... wolf, vampire, omega, damaged, psycho... he doesn't care. As long as I don't leave him behind again, he won't abandon me too.

I vaguely hear Bennet's phone ring so I glance up into the faces of the people in the room. They all look worried or sad when they look at me. Is it my face or am I broadcasting? I don't know, so I try not to think of anything. It's easier said than done. Maybe I should learn that lullaby and hum it...

Bennet's phone rings again and again and he's getting angry at it. It rings again and instead of ignoring it like the last few calls, he answers. He was angry at the phone before, but this time he's put on the polite mask. I know that mask. I hate that mask. It means I have to behave like a grownup even when I was a kid.

The voice on the other line is apparently one that Bennet doesn't know, but I know the voice on the other side. It's Max... I forgot to say goodbye to him this morning, but he still managed to find me. I keep waiting for him to give up on me, but he's been there almost always for me since I met him.

I perk up a bit at the sound of his voice. Out of everyone in the pack, I'd have to say Max is the only one who I think wouldn't care that I'm an abomination. He always knew I was a freak of nature, but now I know why... but I don't think it would matter to him. Bennet talks to him for a few minutes and I just play with Mr. Whiskers' feet while I wait. It's rude to make noise during an important phone call and all the grown up calls are important.

Grandpa Eddie is looking at me like he wants to ask me some questions, but I can tell he really doesn't want to know the answers. He only just now stopped being mad at bio dad. I don't need him to be mad at ghosts, too. Wait... are ghosts real, too? I missed so much out of regular school. Do they even teach that in school?

"Looks like the boy got my family's gift and your curse," Gramps says to Bennet.

I look up at him curiously and ask, "What gift are you talking about? I already know I'm cursed. I'm an omega. Of course, I'm cursed."

Lisa comes back into the room growling. Oh, no. I messed up again. What did I say?

"Omegas are blessings!" she says with conviction. "My Papa, rest his soul, was omega and he blessed our family with nine children who all went on to live wonderful lives."

We all stare at her in a bit of shock as she sits down next to me and hands me a cup of tea. "Never let anyone tell you that you are less than perfect the way you are. Your existence alone is a blessing of fate."

As she pulls me into a gentle hug, so as not to spill the tea in my hand, she continues, "your parents came together for one night, before either should have been able to conceive you, and the fates decided you belong in this world. The evils of the world are caused by the selfish and cruel beings and I am absolutely certain you don't have a selfish bone in your body... unless it's for dessert." She pokes me in the side and gets a little giggle out of me. This woman deserves to be a mother. Why didn't the fates give her a child? I can't help but feel I'm the reason she can't have a kid with Bennet.

"You aren't the reason," Bennet tells me, lifting my chin so he is looking at me eye to eye. "Lisa and I don't lay together. We never have. She lost her fated mate in a tragic accident and joined our pack for a fresh start. We have tried in vitro fertilization, but it just never takes."

"Magic and science don't mix," I whisper. I didn't mean to say it out loud, but at their confused looks... it's time to explain the last eight and a half years of my life.

"How about you start further back?," Gramps asks. "I want to know what happened with you after I left you in the care of Alistair. I need to know."

He looks so sad. I don't want to make him sad. I don't want anyone to be sad. When people are sad, I have to go to the basement... wait, the basement is gone now. Max blew it up with the rocket launcher back in July.

"Maybe we all need to hear this," Bennet says with a growl in his voice.

14

Unburied

Ethan

"Let's start with some cake first, shall we?" Lisa asks as she gets up to grab the box of cupcakes I've been eyeing since we entered the room. They can't be as good as the double chocolate muffins from the coffee shop, but sugar is sugar and Ric doesn't keep much in the house because of Jack. He doesn't understand that all little boys need a regular dose of a sugar rush to be happy... or something. I never got it growing up and I'm trying to give Jack everything I didn't get to have.

After the grownups picked out their dull unfancy cupcakes, Lisa hands me the chocolate one with the electric blue frosting. How did she know that's the one I wanted? She's psychic, has to be. I mean it seems like everyone around me is, so she must be as well.

Her chuckle as she reclaims her seat next to me tells me I'm still broadcasting. Oh, well. It's not like it's a secret in this room.

"Boy, you still need to learn to shield your thoughts for when in other company," Gramps says as he shakes his head.

I look up at him as he takes a bite of his cupcake. He picked vanilla with vanilla frosting - so boring.

Hold up... Vampires eat?

Like real food?

Never woulda guessed.

Does that mean they have to poop too?

How would they deal with the blood then?

Do they just get regular colonoscopy exams or something?

He and Bennet both start coughing and choking on their cupcakes. I guess the vanilla ones must be pretty dry. Lisa snorts next to me.

The doorbell rings and Bennet gets up to answer like he's expecting company. I start to worry about meeting another stranger, when I hear Max's voice float in from the hallway. Max is here? Is he here to bring me home? I hope not. I'm not ready to leave. I just found my birth family, or what's left of it, and I'm not ready to give that up yet.

When Max comes in the room, I can see the relief in his eyes that I'm here and whole, but then his look hardens when he sniffs the air. I think he smells my anxiety.

"You ok, little dude?" he asks me, ducking his head so that he can make sure we have eye contact.

"You're not here to take me back, are you?" I ask him in a whisper. I can feel my sternum bruising from Stabby being pushed into it with how tightly I'm clutching Mr. Whiskers. Max would never do anything to hurt me, but I'm still scared.

"Not unless you want to go back," he says as he sits down on the other side of me and rests his hand on my knee. "Ric doesn't even know I'm here."

Since Max took his spot, Bennet sits across the table on the loveseat and leans forward, "Ethan, I think it's time to tell us what happened to you."

I swallow and don't know where to start. It's too much to tell them all of it. I mean, the stuff in the basement was bad and I know that she shouldn't have done that to a kid, but beyond that, I mean I was a naughty kid so I got into trouble a lot but she only really hurt me in the basement where no one would see.

The four growls in the room bring me out of my thoughts. Shit... still broadcasting.

"How about I share what I know and then you can pick it up with the lab, ok little dude?" Max suggests. I nod and sigh with relief. I know enough to know that the way I grew up was not normal, but I don't know what is important to tell my new family...

As Max starts to tell them, I relax into Lisa's side. She's a good snuggler. I really hope she gets the chance to be a mom someday...

"OK so I didn't meet Ethan until he was about ten, but I've pieced together what he grew up with over the time since I've known him and especially over the last six months or so since we got him back..."

He looks at my father and grandfather... wow so weird to think that... and asks, "how far back do you want me to go?"

"I need to know why my deal with Alistair was broken," Gramps tells him. Bennet nods in agreement and Max takes a second to think before continuing.

"Dunno anything about a deal, but Alpha Alistair was killed in a vicious attack when I was about nine years old or roughly there-about. Alpha Dick... sorry, Richard,"

Pretty sure I will never see a vampire shoot tea out of their nose again in my lifetime. That was pretty funny. But I need to pay attention cuz the papers only gave me the surface details. Max apparently had dug deeper.

"Alpha Richard," he continues with a half smile on his face. He did it on purpose. "had been approached by Esther Sinclair about an urgent matter and less than two days later, Alpha Alistair was dead and the rumor was spread throughout the pack that he died valiantly defending some pups from vampires who were trying to steal and drain them."

Grandpa Eddie lets out a dangerous sounding growl at that, but yeah that tracks with what I figured out except I didn't know fake mom met with Dick beforehand.

"What was the date that he died?" I ask as I'm starting to put things together.

Everyone looks at me, but Max answers honestly, "It was in the spring, so like early May... why?"

"I think it was right after my first trip to the basement," I tell him and his gasp is enough to tell me I think I'm on the right track. "I mean think about it. If Alpha Alistair had a blood oath to a vampire that his grandson wouldn't be harmed and you just did serious harm to the kid, wouldn't you eliminate the person sworn in the blood oath before they can act upon it?"

Why is everyone looking at me like I grew a second head? I told Max about the basement, right? Oh... that's right. I only told Connie about that day. But yeah I kinda remember the people being really sad and then they started ignoring me and all after that.

Can you show me what you're talking about with the basement? Gramps is asking in my head. I figure since he's got these tricks, too he should be able to just pull the memories if I think about them a little bit.

That's right. Just think of the memory and I can pull it. Do you want me to share with everyone or keep it just between us?

I ponder for a second before deciding. *Just share it. Max saw the basement when we were back there. I think it will be good for him to see it not covered in bits of Pete.*

Edward gives me a strange look before he shares my memory of the first time in the basement with the room. I don't need to see it. I lived it. So I just sit licking the frosting off my cupcake waiting for them to get through it all. I bet my tongue is blue now. I wanna find a mirror to check.

Lisa hands me a compact and smiles at me. She's looking a bit paler than before. I hope she's not getting sick... wait, we don't get sick. Or at least I don't. I don't remember if Connie ever caught a cold. He was really the only person I was ever around in the house and outside of the house it was Max and Ric and Connie or Shaun before he moved away.

Oh...

They're all looking at me.

15

———

Unburied

Ethan

"Is there something on my face?" I ask trying to lick around my mouth to catch any frosting I might have missed. That seems to break the weird tension that I was feeling and Bennet even chuckles a bit.

"So yeah," Max says. "I'm pretty sure we just found out the why. If Alistair was blood oathed to ensure Ethan's safety, he would have been duty bound to kill Esther for what she did that day. Blaming vampires and saying they threatened pups basically ensured that no one from the pack would seek you out or tell you anything about our pack."

Wow... fake mom went to a lot of trouble just to be able to play doctor with me. *But why did she even keep me after that?*

"To keep up appearances, little dude," Max says. Oops, I guess I sent that out. He nods to me but continues, "From what I saw, the Sinclairs were all about appearances. Connor had to get the top grades and be the best at sports and have the nicest toys and clothes. Mr. Sinclair drove the nicest cars and went to play golf with the Alpha twice a week. Mrs. Sinclair had all of the ladies events and was the perfect stay at home mom. At least that was the appearance they wanted to present to the world."

He looks sad when he turns to me and says, "You were the complication they didn't plan for. John pretended you just didn't exist until someone asked about you. I don't know what Esther's problem was but it seemed like she actively hated you and probably would have killed you as an infant if she could have gotten away with it. But once it was established in the pack that you were their second kid, they had to keep up appearances."

Well now. That actually fits. I always wondered why they could go from being so nice to being nightmares, but now it makes a bit more sense. I should have seen it earlier. It's why I liked the fancy dinners and stuff when I got to go. It meant I got the loving mommy like on tv… It kind of hurts worse than thinking I was just a mistake to them. To know I just flat out meant nothing…

"Connor was their golden boy and they kept him in the dark about the way they treated Ethan," Max explains to everyone in the room. I know all of this, but it's still painful to know that my big brother was right there and saw nothing, heard nothing… all because he had it so good he couldn't imagine anyone not living the good life in our pack, let alone our house.

"Like I said before, I met Ethan when he was ten. It was after school and I saw a bunch of pups beating on something. I ran them off, seeing as how I was a big old scary teenager and all. I thought it would be a cat or puppy or some other small animal that they were trying to kill, but no it was little dude here" As he nods his head toward me, I duck away and grab for another cupcake. I don't like being the center of attention, but it's better that he tells the stories.

"I took him to my place, which was only marginally safer than the side street I found him on, and cleaned him up and went to bandage him up only to find there were no wounds. He was freaking out that he would get in trouble for the blood on his clothes but there were no wounds."

I can hear their reactions to Max's words, but I'm trying to not hear them. I just want to concentrate on my cupcake. I can't decide if the purple icing tastes different than the blue. Do the colors really taste different or is it just in my head?

"I was freaked out by that but got him changed and gave him my favorite switchblade for defense and showed him how to use it. I even told him to find me after he used it so I could show him how to clean up. It was less than two weeks later that he found me for clean up. It wasn't until much later that I found out that the adults of the pack turned the other way when he was getting bullied and attacked. I found out that the parents of those pups were actually encouraging them to try and kill him for some reason."

I look up at the growls I can hear coming from the other three in the room. They all look really angry, so I grab a third cupcake. This time I want to see if the purple icing tastes the same on the dry ass vanilla cakes...

"My mom was high most of the time when she wasn't whoring herself out, or trying to whore me out, so we never really paid attention to the other drama in the pack before. I didn't notice until literally stumbling upon him that day."

Max never shared that with me before. I freeze mid-lick of the purple icing and look at him. I knew he saw me, but he never said anything about his mom doing that. Is that why he knows what to do with me when I hurt? Is that why he was so hurt back in July after my heat?

"I'm sorry!" I say as I throw my arms around his neck to give him a hug, smacking him in the face with the half licked cupcake.

None of us can stop the laughter that bubbles up when I pull away to reveal a streak of purple that starts in front of his left ear and goes through his hair to the back of his head. "Oops..."

"No problemo, dude," he says as Bennet hands him a napkin to wipe himself off. "My life was shit and I own that and deal with the aftermath every day. Therapy helped, but it was still a shit way to grow up."

Max went to therapy? A strong guy like him did it? Maybe I should think about it more, but not yet. I'm not ready yet. Just the thought of the d-word makes me break out in a cold sweat. No white coats for me...

"So after meeting him, I asked around and apparently a rumor got put out there that Ethan was an abomination and was attacked by vampires when Alpha Alistair was killed and his blood was polluted or something and that's why everyone hated on a little kid. I went to ask the Alpha to put a stop to it, thinking he'd do the right thing since he was a dad and all, but he just ignored me as a punk kid. I was from the wrong side of the tracks and all that. He was a regular customer of my mom's but again, appearances mattered more than the truth in the Jameson pack under Alpha Richard."

That's why they all hated me? They thought I survived a vampire attack and still proceeded to treat me like that?! That's like blaming a girl for walking down her street and getting raped by a passerby. What in the fuck is wrong with people!?

Max pulls me against his side to settle me down. I need it. I could understand hating the vampire blood, but I was a kid... and a supposed victim... I'm glad they're all dead now. Max smiles down at me and kisses the top of my head before continuing.

"At that point, I did the only thing I could to protect the kid. I became friends with his older brother and by proxy, the Alpha's son. I needed to make sure they weren't abusing him as well, but nah… they were just dumb teenagers, focused on school and sports and girls, sometimes guys. Our wolves tend to be fluid like that and all…"

He gives me another half smile and a squeeze. I like having the big lug around again. It feels a bit safer to be the real me when he's here.

"But they looked at Ethan as a tag-a-long most of the time and basically only tolerated him when others were around. Yeah, they'd ditch him, but never in an unsafe place and never in a way that would hurt him. They cared about him a lot when no one else from school was around, so I came to genuinely befriend the two of them."

He gets a faraway look in his eyes and continues, "It was like a dream being friends with them. I got to keep an eye on the little dude, yeah, but for a while even I stopped watching out for him. It was so nice to be noticed for something positive. It was like heaven being away from my house and my Ma and everything going on there. I didn't realize just how much I missed in retrospect, just by being able to enjoy life for the first time."

There's a weight to the pause, like none of us want to interrupt. This time I give Max a squeeze. He did his best to help me back then… I know he did.

He manages to shake off whatever he's thinking about and continues to explain to us all what he knows.

16

Ethan

"From what I could tell, life in the Sinclair house was drastically different for Ethan when Connor was home compared to when he wasn't," Max explains to the others in the room. I am already well aware of how different it was if Connie wasn't there.

"If Connor or Ric were present, the worst Ethan would suffer was being ignored. If they weren't at the house and there were no adults around, Ethan was degraded and treated like less than a dog, less than a slave."

He takes a deep breath and I can tell he's fighting his anger from coming out...

"I once saw Esther smack him across the face for tripping on the rug and making too much noise during her show. She saw me. I didn't matter, so she didn't bother to hide it. After all, who would take the word of the whore's son over her own?"

He's shaking in his anger. I didn't know he actually saw any of it. I don't like that he saw it. It didn't hurt as much knowing that the people who I love didn't see it. Max saw it and he couldn't do anything. Mom would have... not Mom... fake mom... Esther... she would have destroyed him, gotten him kicked out of the pack...

Lisa pulls me away from Max into her arms for a hug. Max gives me a tense smile and a squeeze on my thigh before he continues on. He seems to be back in control, but I can see the storm in his eyes.

"This is what I've found out in the last six months:" he leads into telling us all he found out.

"The day of Ethan's thirteenth birthday, Richard, Esther, and John all conspired to make sure that Ric and Connor would be out of town for the day. The college trip being scheduled for that day was planned to make sure there was no time for Connor or Ric to figure out a way to reschedule it again. Esther had taken care of that part.

"See, Richard had arranged for someone to pick up Ethan that night after ten and then Esther and John were supposed to set the fire that night and say they barely made it out alive.

"Apparently, Carl Welling, Esther's brother, managed to find out their plan and wanted his cut for keeping silent. He went over that night and ended up fighting John and killing him."

HOLD UP! Uncle Carl is the one who killed Dad...erm... John? Alpha Dick didn't set up the lab? Did I make Ric hate his father for nothing? Was I all wrong in what I found? Oh, Daddy is gonna be so mad at me...

Max grabs my hand that isn't crushing Mr. Whiskers to my chest and grips it tight before he goes on to explain.

"From what I understand, Carl is the one who took Ethan and when the people who Richard set up to take him showed up to find Ethan wasn't there, they killed Esther and set the fire. She was still knocked out from whatever Carl had used to knock Ethan out. There was no body to represent Ethan in the house. Richard dug one up from the cemetery and charred it for when Connor went to identify…"

He pauses and seems haunted by the memories. Gramps is apparently following along in his head because he's wiping at tears under his own eyes. I don't want to ever see the images of what Connie had to go through. If I did, I probably wouldn't be able to keep to the G Lady's no killing rule.

"Based on what I found, that's the reason Carl didn't move with the pack when we all up and relocated to here. Carl double crossed his sister and his Alpha, but Richard couldn't exact any type of revenge without revealing his own dirty dealings, so he excommunicated Carl and just left him here in the old Welling house by himself."

I always wondered why Uncle Carl stayed behind. I thought he was like a liaison for Alpha Dick. I guess he was flying solo instead…

"As for what happened next with Ethan, I don't know all of the details and by the Goddess, I don't want to know. I just know that once we were here, Richard got paranoid as fuck and built up the pack like we would be going to war at any moment. I trained hard to become a warrior and worked my way up the ranks to the point I was second in command before I even turned twenty one.

"Then one day we all wake up to the news that the Alpha and his mate are dead from a car crash…that their car flew off a cliff due to speed and they both perished along with the head of the warriors who was driving."

He looks sad and a little confused, like this has been eating away at him for the past five years.

"I knew the guy who was ahead of me. He was my mentor… he took the safety of the Alpha's family way too seriously. Like, he needed the stick surgically removed from his ass seriously…

"There's no way he was speeding. Maybe if it was just Richard in the car, but not Annabelle. He would have never risked his sister like that. He would have never risked her not getting home to Jack...

"Anyways, after that day, Ric was Alpha and I was head warrior and Connor was Beta and the pack just shuffled on... until finding out Ethan wasn't dead and all of the proof found in the houses of the old pack shook things up to the point that all of the old pack that was complicit have been taken care of."

17

Unburied

I kinda shake myself back awake. Most of what Max just told everyone is stuff I already know - although the stuff about how Ric's mom passed is kind of surprising to me.

She was always really nice to me, even when everyone else was mean or indifferent. She always tried to sneak me sweets when I got dragged to the fancy events. She would try to talk to me, but fake mom never let me talk to anyone. I hope she didn't suffer. She was a nice lady and a good mom. Jackie should've gotten to grow up with a good mom like her.

Gramps gets up and walks out of the room towards the kitchen. I don't really understand why he's so upset right now. He hasn't even heard the bad stuff yet. I mean, Max doesn't know the stuff from the lab except the deal.

Oh yeah, I should probably tell them about the deal...

Hey Grandpa Eddie? Can you pull the memory about the deal from my head? I send towards the kitchen. I know he hasn't left yet, but he's not a DVD player so it's only polite to ask.

He's chuckling as he comes back in the room wiping at his eyes.

Why was he crying?

Was it still because of seeing Connie when he thought I was dead? Yeah, I don't want to see that memory, ever…

"Show me this deal and I'll share it with everyone," he says out loud, I guess to prepare everyone that he's going to be blasting their brains again.

"Don't need to show me," Max says. "I already saw it once and I'm still pissed about it."

He's pissed? Why is he pissed? The Goddess made sure I made it out alive. They couldn't kill me because of her deal. It's all a good thing overall… I mean the baby thing was a bitch move, but I couldn't live with myself if I lost Connie.

"What baby thing?" Max asks while they're all in the middle of the memory.

Crap… No one is supposed to know about the baby. Ric will be so sad if he finds out about the details about the baby. He'll never forgive me then.

For now, I at least still have a chance to go back eventually, but not if he finds out about the baby. I won't be welcome back ever again if he finds out… or rather, I won't be his little Blue anymore and that thought hurts worse than the thought of not going back.

Everyone is looking at me. Lisa looks sad. All the guys look angry.

"Please tell me you have a way to break this deal," Bennet says into the tense silence of the room.

"Only by giving breath to new life," I say trying to imitate the breathy voice of the Goddess. "Basically, I gotta pop out a living kid and then I'm free." Free of the deal. Free of her protections.

Free to not hold back anymore and kill if I have to.

Free to have a family without fear...

There's a look in Bennet's eyes that I can't define. He looks guilty, but I'm not sure what for. I glance to Grampa Eddie and see a look of shock on his face. Max is just as confused as I am as Lisa pulls me into her side to hold me tight.

"What am I missing here?" I ask. They know something. Secrets. More secrets. Why is it always secrets around me???

"How about we resume this in a few hours?" Lisa suggests pointing toward the window with a nod of her chin. "Or better yet, we reconvene after we all get some sleep?"

Holy crap, it's getting light outside. It's morning already? Wait... I have classes today. I can't miss class...

But Daddy is paying for them. If I keep going, am I going to have to pay? Do I need to get a job? I don't have the rhythm to be a stripper...

"You are most definitely my son," Bennet chuckles as he puts his hands under my arms and lifts me to stand. "Don't worry about your classes. Your tuition is covered whether Jameson pays it or not."

At his statement, Max just about chokes on his own tongue... "Son?" He looks at me in amazement and I nod with a smile. The big lug jumps up from the sofa and crushes me in a hug that is just the right side of too tight. "I'm so happy for you, little one," he whispers into my ear.

Bennet leads him down the hall towards what I assume is his office with them chatting about whatever. Lisa stands up next to me and says she's going to go make up a couple more rooms for our guests. I guess Max is staying, but I look at Edward and ask, "Won't you burn up in the sun?"

He laughs a full throated and joyous sound that makes me smile. "No I won't burn up in the sun. It just feels like a really annoying sunburn to me at my age if I'm exposed to direct sunlight, but it's not deadly."

"We have a lightproof room for when he or one of the others come to visit on business," Lisa says from the top of the steps. "Come on Ethan, let me get you a towel and some pajamas so you can take a bath and get to bed."

Oooh! A bath! Too bad I don't have my tubby toys here.

Maybe Lisa will be ok with me getting some for when I come back to visit...

18

Ric

Ethan's been gone for over a day now. It's officially been over twenty four hours since I've seen him, spoken to him, heard his laugh… This hasn't happened since he woke up after the incident. I stand in front of the coffee maker staring. What am I going to do with his coffee if he doesn't come home?

The sound of the front door snaps me out of the funk I've fallen into. I push the button to brew my cup and turn toward the entrance of my kitchen to see Connor standing there with a very confused look on his face. I didn't tell him anything about yesterday. Considering he collapsed from exhaustion, I let him rest at home while I was working to find a way to bring my boy back home. Perhaps, judging by the look on his face, I was mistaken in doing that.

"Why the fuck is my brother not home?" he asks me, setting the mail down on the counter.

I don't answer him. Instead, my eyes are fixed on an envelope that just slid from the center of the pile of mail just enough to show me that it is addressed in Ethan's handwriting. I snatch it up and run to my office to read it in private. I don't want my Beta to know how badly I screwed things up this time. I don't need anyone else to see what my boy has to say.

But of course, Connor follows and doesn't let himself be locked out. He plants himself in the very chair that Ethan was in yesterday morning and refuses to leave.

"Talk to me," he says. I can tell he's holding something back, but I explain as best I can what happened the day before. His eyes reveal everything. He is furious with me, just as Max was. But this is my best friend, and he always has my back. I finish telling him everything, including that Jack opted to spend another night at his friend's house when he found out Ethan hadn't come back yet.

"You are an unmitigated ass," my Beta sighs. I can't really deny that fact, but at least he didn't storm out. "My brother is now in the pack of another Alpha, one I don't know at all thanks to your vampire prejudice, and you're telling me that I can't even go to visit him without risking war?"

Well, I hadn't considered that. Bennet wouldn't risk a war for Connor wanting to see his brother, right? I mean, I don't know the man well at all, only having seen him while my father was still alive, but he wouldn't be so cruel as to cut away all of Ethan's family...

"Give me Alpha Heartstone's number so that I can get permission to see my brother," Connor demands of me. "I just got him back and I refuse to have your stupidity and pride cost me my relationship with him."

Just how badly did I screw up here? This is the second of my closest people that has turned on me in favor of my mate. Don't get me wrong, I'm extremely thankful Ethan has them, but it brings into question how much of my pack is actually loyal to *me*...

I slide my phone over to him so that he can get the number while I open the letter. Maybe I can get through it while he's distracted and then I can digest it all in private.

Dear Daddy,

I guess it should be Alpha Alaric now. I'm sorry I brought so much trouble to your pack, to your life. I'm sorry I put Jack in danger by being there. That was never my intention. I only wanted to get a muffin, but apparently the fates are intent on making sure I don't get anything good in my life.

I shouldn't have ditched class. I shouldn't have used my speed to get away from Seb. Don't blame him. There's no way he would have seen me even had he not had to pee.

I shouldn't have interfered in another pack's business, but those betas were harassing human women and getting physical when they said no. I had to say something! I didn't expect them to sneak up on me when I went back to get my coffee.

I didn't mean to end up in a vampire's office. I didn't mean to make one of my messes. I didn't mean to injure another pack's wolves like that. I didn't mean to want to steal a new stabby bit from the vampires.

I didn't want any of it to happen, but it's my fault for skipping class. Now, you are all in danger from the vampires and from the Heartstone pack and it's all because of me. So now, I'm going to fix it.

I don't know if I'll be able to come back to you after all of this, or even if you'll want me to. After reading this, you're probably going to want to find a new boy or a nice

The letter falls from my hands as I sit back staring at the ceiling. I'm not even trying to hold back the tears that fall from my eyes. Connor can see my pain... Hell, the whole world can see my pain. I don't care anymore. My boy thinks he's a burden and a danger to us, and it's all my fault.

I vaguely notice Connor grab the letter from the floor and read it. The look he gives me is one I deserve. I failed. I horribly failed. Maybe he is better off away from me. Maybe it's time for me to let go and just stop trying to be a man worthy of such a gift. Maybe it's time for me to just be the Alpha and forget everything else. My heart won't ever come back from this, so perhaps it's time to just let that part of me die...

The slap across my face is completely unexpected and my wolf rises to the surface with a growl.

"What in the actual fuck, Connor?!" I growl at him.

"Get your damn head out of your ass and figure out a way to get my brother back, you stupid selfish piece of shit!"

The front door slams hard enough to shake the walls of my office. A few pictures fall off the wall. They aren't important ones. I manage to grab the one from Christmas before it falls. The joy on Ethan's face shines through. It was his first real holiday. His first time getting presents that were truly for him. I will do anything to bring that joy back to his face, the light back to his baby blues.

Seeing my phone on the desk, I steel myself to swallow my pride and try to reach out.

Knowing that Alpha Bennet won't answer if I call, I send a text message.

> I'm not trying to interfere with the sanctuary you have granted my mate. Does his brother have your permission to visit him?
>
> He is distraught at the thought of being kept from his little brother.

Sending that message hurts. I know if Ethan decides to stay in the Heartstone pack, I will lose my Beta. Connor won't stay here without Ethan... not after everything we found out about how his parents treated him as a child. Connor never told me what Ethan showed him that day at the old pack, but I read the journals. I know what the bitch did.

My phone ringing surprises me. I didn't think the Alpha would call me... it's Max.

"Jack is staying another night," I tell him before he can say anything. That's the only reason I can think of for Max to be calling me this early. The sun is barely up.

"Sorry, Bossman. That's not why I'm calling," he tells me. "Alpha Heartstone wanted me to pass along the message that little dude has the final say in who can visit and that anyone looking for permission can contact me and I'll find out if the little dude wants to see them."

Wait... what?

"Why are you running messages for the Alpha of another

pack?" I growl to him over the phone. My wolf doesn't like the fact that our head warrior is playing lackey to someone else.

"Knock it off, asshole," he growls back at me. "I'm here for Ethan. Always have been. You've had your head so far up your own ass for your entire life while this kid was fighting to survive. He's the one who needs me, not you!"

My wolf stops in shock. I'm dumbfounded as well. Max has never been loyal to me? But for those eight years...

"So why did you stay when we all thought he was gone? Why were you here at all if you didn't care about me or the pack?"

I need to know why. I count this man as a brother, but has he never seen it that way?

"Because of Jack," he says. "You'd already proven you couldn't see the evils around you and I wasn't going to let another kid in your circle suffer."

Next thing I know, I'm listening to silence. I look down to see he has disconnected the call. In a daze, I make my way back to the kitchen to the now cold cup of coffee I abandoned earlier. I dump it out in the sink and make another cup. At the first sip, I can't stop the tears.

I grabbed the wrong pod.

This is Ethan's coffee.

Ethan

I know I should get more sleep than this, but I just can't get comfortable in this bed. Yeah, Mr. Whiskers is a great snuggler, but he needs to fatten back up a bit because Stabby keeps poking me in the ribs... not with the pointy end though. That would be bad. No, Stabby's pointy end stays secure just like Max showed me all those years ago.

I didn't know that's how Max saw me back then. I thought he

was always Connie's friend, and Ric's friend. Everyone wanted to be their friends but they were very selective. But it turns out, Max has been *my* friend all along. That's news to me and I'm not sure how I feel about it. Does that mean Max is going to be staying with me if I stay here?

No! He can't do that! He needs to be back in the Jameson pack to protect Jack! He's special like me. He needs to be protected. The bad men are going to get him if Max isn't there. I need to stop the bad men! I need to go!

In my rush to put some clothes on, I guess I have Lisa to thank for the clean clothes, I end up falling over. Pants legs are much more difficult when you're in a rush. I guess the sound woke people up because my door suddenly opens to reveal three very anxious men, who obviously just woke up.

I can't hold back the giggle at how they look. Grandpa Eddie's shirt is inside out and backwards, the tag sitting under his chin just waving at us all. How can he even stand to wear shirts with tags in them? Doesn't it itch? Anyways... Max has a major cowlick situation going on the side of his head... is that purple? Did he forget to wash out the icing from the cupcake?

My giggle fit intensifies as they are all looking at each other in confusion. I guess they finally see what I do and they all share a bit of a chuckle and wait for me to calm down.

"Where you off to in such a hurry, little dude?" Max asks me once I can breathe without dissolving back into laughter.

That sobers me up immediately. "I have to go," I tell them. "I have to stop the bad men before they come for Jackie. If you aren't there with Jackie, they'll get him and I can't let that happen. They can't have him. They can't take his sunshine."

Max snatches me into a hug, pressing my face into his broad chest. It's not as good as a Daddy hug, but it's pretty nice in its own way.

"No one is going to take Jackie anywhere," he growls out. "Seb and Bastian both are watching him while I'm here with you."

But Seb is who I slipped by to start all of this... Is he observant enough to stop the bad men, to see the bad men?

This time I'm fully aware I'm thinking too loud but don't really care. Jackie's safety is more important than anything else.

My boy, your little brother is safe as can be. I have my own men watching over your pack in your absence. I hear Grandpa Eddie's voice in my head.

"My pack?" I ask as I look at him in the doorway. He's fixed his shirt and somehow managed to braid his hair while Max was hugging me.

"As the mate of the Alpha, the pack is as much yours as it is his," says Lisa, pushing her way through the men to bring a steaming cup of coffee to me. "Your word is law and can only be contradicted by the Alpha himself."

I didn't know that. Ms. Annabelle, Ric's mother, didn't act like that. Hell, most of the pack looked at her and treated her as just a piece of arm candy... the Alpha certainly did. It's why she was able to be so nice to me. No one paid her any attention unless the Alpha needed a photo op.

Why does Gramps look a bit green again? Should he not have eaten the cupcakes last night? I think towards Lisa. She seems to be the one person here who might actually know things who isn't going to have a reaction to my ignorance.

I don't know why, sweetie. He can eat food just fine, so I think it's the subject of the conversation or maybe someone's thoughts that is affecting him.

Thoughts? Come to think of it, he was like this last night when Max was talking about when Ms. Annabelle died with Alpha Richard and the warrior dude. What was his name again? Alex... Alan...

"Aaron. His name was Aaron," Gramps says to me as he looks down at the floor.

"I guess I should tell you since I'm apparently shit at holding back my reactions about this subject," he says.

I'm intrigued, so I sit on the edge of the bed, criss cross applesauce, and sip my coffee like it's a long awaited story time... Oh this coffee is just perfect. Lisa smiles at me as she hands me Mr. Whiskers and sits next to me to listen. Yeah.. she's my new mom. It's official. I don't think my bio mom would be mad at that. I used to think maybe the Goddess messed up and my mom should have been Ms. Annabelle but now I realize that would've been really bad with Ric and me being mates and all.

Gramps chuckles a bit before turning serious again. "It started with the deal with Alistair," he says.

"I didn't know Richard was in charge as long as he was. I thought Alistair had betrayed me. I knew they had relocated here, but I was concerned for finding my nephew and never wanted to look at the faces of those that failed to keep you alive. I was out for vengeance on those that took my heir from me, and was going to revisit vengeance for you upon the one who broke his oath once I knew Joshua was safe.

"I only found out Alistair was dead when you turned sixteen and your blood called out to me. At that time, I visited the Jameson pack and saw that Richard was in charge. I was going to confront him, but his mate came up to him carrying a babe. The innocence shone off both her and the babe, so I left. I didn't look deeper. I just refocused my efforts to finding Joshua. I hoped you were just in hiding since it was obvious you weren't there. In a million years, I never would have expected you to be in the situation you were forced into. I thought you were sent away because someone found out about our connection and wanted to use you against me..."

He pauses in his story to look at me. I guess my confusion is showing on my face because he smiles and begins elaborating.

"Vampire blood matures or comes of age at sixteen. That's when the full strength of our abilities truly manifest, but we will always have at least a bit of them kick in at puberty. That is why you could only speak into someone's mind but not hear a response at that age. That is why you were faster than a normal wolf, but hadn't yet developed the speed of our people.

"When you turned sixteen, your blood woke up fully and called to me. That was when I knew you were alive and hadn't died like Alpha Richard had intended me to believe. As for Joshua, he is my vampire heir that I chose when I was told you had died. He didn't appreciate it. He thought that the mantle of leadership wouldn't fall to him with him being the fourth son in a three region kingdom... And he ran away only to find himself in a situation he didn't expect."

Ok that makes a bit more sense now. But I'm still confused.

"What does that have to do with their car accident and... and..." I can't bring myself to ask. I don't want to know the answer. I have to ask. I have to know. If there's a chance that this man is not going to be here for me in the future, I have to know now. Am I a shiny new thing to be abandoned or am I truly and permanently here... I can't let him in if he's going to forget about me...

"You are my grandson!" he growls in apparent frustration. "Now that I've found you again, you'll never be rid of me. Not even if you want it."

I beam at him through the tears. I didn't know that's the answer I wanted, but it was the right one. I've never felt what they refer to as unconditional love. Is that what this is? Is this happiness something I can actually count on getting to feel again? Butterflies are exploding inside me... wait that's a bit grotesque. But yeah, I can't think of a better explanation...

"I will always love you, my little wolf," Grandpa Eddie whispers to me as he leans down to give me a kiss on the forehead. I like that nickname a lot.

"Same goes for us," Bennet says indicating himself and Lisa who nods at me from her place beside me.

I have a family! This is awesome! I can't wait to tell Daddy...

My heart sinks. All the butterflies have turned to swamp water. I don't feel so good now.

Max sits on my other side and pulls me into his side when the tears start to fall again. I want my Daddy, but he doesn't want a troublemaker like me... he promised to love me, too and I only end up making him angry and sad. I don't want to make my new family sad, too. I should just go so they can stay happy...

I'm surrounded by growling and it shocks me into looking around the room. Four hard faces are staring at me. I knew it was too good to be true. Fate doesn't let me be happy. I used up all of the happiness I'm allowed to have at Christmas. It's time to go before I take their happiness too.

I try to stand up, but Max won't let go of me. I try again, and Lisa's hand grabs mine while Bennet kneels in front of me with his hands on both my knees. Why won't they let me go? I'm only going to cause them pain. It's already happening.

"Please," I beg them. "Please just let me go. I don't want to hurt anyone else."

Lisa gets up and leaves the room in tears. I'm glad. She's a nice lady and if I'm not around, she should be able to get to be a mom finally. She deserves that. But the three men in the room don't seem to want to leave. Why don't they understand that I only ever bring pain?

"You can't hurt us," Bennet tells me, still kneeling in front of me. "The only thing you can do to hurt us is to leave us again. We love you and to lose you would be like cutting out our own hearts."

He stands and takes Lisa's place by my side, pulling me from Max's arms into his own.

"As for physically hurting us, you can't cause us lasting damage," he says, rocking me side to side. It feels kinda nice. "The reason I hoped you could break the deal with the Goddess is because it's a lopsided deal in her favor. You don't need to worry about death, regardless of her deal."

At that, my head lifts up so fast I end up smacking into his chin. What does he mean I don't have to worry about death? I'm seeing stars from the new bump on my head, but this is more important. What the fuck does that mean?

Bennet spits out a broken tooth before continuing, keeping his head tilted toward the ceiling. I guess he's trying to avoid another busted tooth. Can't say I blame him... My head is pounding a bit from the contact.

"My mother's line, my line, your line," he says glancing down at me. "We're cursed, or blessed... depends on who you ask. But long story short, because of a witch and some sort of love triangle long ago, we can't die unless our head or heart is removed or destroyed. It only affects the firstborn son of each generation... which would be you."

While I'm sitting here with my whole world imploding, he keeps talking. I kinda hear it, but I'll have to rely on my brain to clue me in on the important parts later.

"didn't know Lizzie was... then no one said anything about... we all thought... lifted... no one else ..."

I should probably clue back in at some point, but all I can think about is that my grandfather knew I was alive at sixteen. My father is the reason I didn't die. I was trapped in that place for a whole year after they knew I was alive. The G Lady took advantage of my blood and my abilities to make a deal with me that I didn't need... or did I? I didn't want to get pregnant and I didn't get pregnant, so she kept up at least part of the bargain, right?

"Little dude?" Max interrupts my stream of thoughts. I look over to him and see a look I never expected to see from him. Why is he giving me that look? Max doesn't pity anyone. He shows them how to be stronger. He doesn't pity...

There are tears in his eyes as he starts talking. The rest of the room is silent.

"You wouldn't have gotten pregnant," he tells me, not breaking eye contact.

"Yeah, I know. It's the only thing the G Lady really did for me," I respond, not knowing why everyone is surprised by that.

"You weren't marked or claimed," Max says to me softly.

"Yeah," I reply, drawing out the word into a question. "Most everyone that had a go was human. The few supes that did were forced and none of us wanted a permanent reminder of that place."

Max hides his face in his hands. Is he crying? Max doesn't cry.

I look up to see horror on Bennet's face and pure rage on Grandpa Eddie's face.

"What am I missing?" I ask. There's something I'm just not getting here... something I apparently should already know. Why am I so stupid?

Ignorance is not the same as stupidity. Gramps sends to my head. *One is a lack of opportunity. The other is a lack of willingness to learn.*

"They teach it in high school," Max groans from behind his hands. "Ninth grade health, or maybe tenth... it's our sex ed course. We all thought it was the most useless class and mostly goofed off. But the gist of it is, as a wolf, an omega or female, you can't get pregnant unless you're with your mate, fated or claimed. Since Ric is your fated mate, you couldn't get knocked up by anyone in there unless they claimed you."

My heart stops and my breathing stutters... The G Lady played me? Has she done anything for me at all?

My wolf starts growling and I can't contain it inside. My growl echoes through the room and the three men are all on edge.

She did nothing, yet took from us, my wolf growls to me. It takes me a second to realize what he's talking about.

Oh...OH!

That. Fucking. BITCH!

My wolf bursts out of me and next thing I know I'm in the woods heading for my cave. I don't feel the cold in this form, but I am a bit concerned at how I left the house and Heartstone territory. I really hope I didn't hurt anyone when I left.

19

Unburied

Ric

It's been a full month since my boy left me... since everyone left me. Jack came home for about an hour. He packed some clothes and decided he's living at this friend's house until I fix things with Ethan. Oh to be an eight year old again and believe anything can be fixed...

Connor isn't much better though. Apparently, he got a letter at the Beta house from Ethan. I don't know what his letter said, but my Beta only talks to me about security and business... and most of that comes through Seb. I've lost my best friend, my brother, and my mate because of my stupid pride.

My warriors aren't any help either. Max hasn't been back since the night he called Bennet, and the men have noticed. They are following the lead of their head warrior and seem to be avoiding me. I only ever get quick updates and then they're gone. Seb and Bastian and the others don't hang around anymore.

It's abundantly clear now that I am an asshole and that I was in the wrong that morning. I want to fix it, but I just don't know where to start. I can't reach out to my mate without starting a war. I can't risk the pack for one person, can I? I want to. Oh gods know I want to. I need my little Blue like I need oxygen, but he would hate me even more if I went to him now. He left because he thought he was keeping us all safe. I can't put us all in danger to get him back, right?

The ache in my chest doesn't go away now. I can't bring myself to toss out Ethan's favorite foods, even if they've gone bad in his absence. I have to make a cup of his coffee every day, even though I hate the taste of it. I can't stand the thought of seeing my pods decreasing in number while his stay the same. I don't need the visual reminder every morning. I'm reminded enough waking up alone in our bed.

Sipping the disgusting coffee, I walk out to the gate to grab the mail. Posted on the wrought iron is a thick envelope that looks like some of the edges have burned a bit... that's strange. Why didn't they just put it in the mailbox? And what's the deal with the decorative charring?

I take everything into my office and start to open the mail. This has become my routine. The house that was full of life and laughter is now dull and silent. The only thing I can do is work. Some of the she-wolves dropped by in the beginning, but they finally got the message that there is no other mate for me but my bluebird.

I didn't think the pack still disrespected him so much, but I made quick work of that situation. They all know that their choice is to accept and respect my mate or to get the fuck out of my pack. Last I heard, three she-wolves have moved away from the area after being rejected by the Heartstone pack for relocation. One was sent back to us, beaten pretty bloody with a note detailing how she had offended the Alpha's mate and that if another she-wolf tries to defect to their pack, it will have consequences for our entire pack.

I turn my attention back to the mail.

Bill... Bill... Bill...

Ethan didn't take his cards, but his wallet and backpack were both gone a few days after he left. I don't know if he took them or if someone else came and got them for him. I don't even know when they went missing, but it was just another sign that my boy isn't planning on coming home anytime soon.

There's nothing of interest or worry in the regular mail, so I pick up the weird envelope. I can feel the energy coming off of it. Active magic has a feel to it, almost like that charge in the air before a thunderstorm. Except multiply that by about a thousand and you'd get what this envelope is giving off. It is sealed with a wax seal, the emblem is an acorn.

Why in the hell am I getting correspondence from the damn Fae royalty from Atlanta? Between the magic and the seal, it can only be them. My father had me memorize all the fae seals before he died.

Opening the letter proves difficult. It won't budge. It's not until I give myself a damn papercut and get blood on the wax that it unseals. There's a pop in the air as the tension in the room floats away. Fucking magic letter bullshit. This is why no one wants to deal with the fae.

Alpha Jameson,

You may be unaware, but you are in possession of something that is rightfully the property of our Prince Kestion.

We seek the return of his property on the grounds

that refusal would be tantamount to a declaration of war.

By the laws that govern us all and the treaties dictating our mutual survival in this world, theft of our property is punishable by death.

Return him to us and we shall show you mercy. You have a fortnight to comply.

Respectfully,
Eldred
First assistant to Prince Kestion of the Unseelie Sidhe

What in the actual fuck?! Who the fuck in my pack could ever be considered property of the fae? I don't have any fae or fae-blooded members of my pack. No one new has come in except...

No.

No fucking way.

The time for the childish picking sides is over. This is about Ethan's safety and wellbeing. I pick up my phone and press to connect the call.

It rings out to voicemail. I try again.

Voicemail again.

Damnit, Bennet! Answer your damn phone!

I keep calling. I don't care how annoying it is. This is life or death.

It takes hours but finally, he picks up.

"What the fuck do you want, Jameson?" he snarls. "My son is not going back to you!"

Son?! His son? What the fuck did I miss?

"Never mind the family dynamics," I say putting it aside for now. Ethan's family saga isn't important at this moment. "Why would the fae think they have a claim on Ethan?"

I'm met with silence and have to pull my phone from my ear to make sure the call is still connected.

"Why are you asking this?" he asks carefully. He knows something, but I'm apparently not going to know what unless I can answer his questions. I'll go through the fucking inquisition if it means keeping my boy safe.

"I had a letter fastened to my gate this morning saying I have two weeks to return their property or it's war," I tell him.

"Fuck!" Is that Max I hear in the background? What the fuck is he doing there?

"Your restriction from my territory has been lifted... temporarily," Bennet says with a note of sadness in his voice. "Come to my house. We need to talk about this, your father, and how we're going to protect my son."

As the call disconnects, I hear Edward in my head, *You might have hurt him in your ignorance and pride, but if you care for him even in the slightest, you will behave and fall in line for this.*

I can't agree more. I will destroy myself completely if it means keeping my bluebird safe.

Ethan

Living in the cave wasn't so bad when I was a wolf, but even in South Carolina, late winter isn't good weather for camping as a person. I lasted a couple of days before I asked Lisa if she knew of somewhere I could stay. Of course, she wanted me to stay at their house, but I really just need some time to myself right now, to get over what all has been taken from me.

I know I should be thankful that I'm here and alive and that I've found my family and they love me...

Trust me, I'm super thankful about all of that.

But why did the fates have to take my mother from me? Why didn't anyone let my father know about me? Why didn't my grandfather take me and raise me? Why was I left with those horrible people in that horrible pack and then sold like a piece of furniture to the highest bidder?

All I had done was be born...

I blink away the tears as I walk into the science building on campus. Lisa had gotten me set up in the dorms, so that I can still attend school and use the canteen and focus on just being me for a while. She's been looking after Mr. Whiskers for me while I'm here. I had a minor freakout over the thought that they wouldn't let me have him in my room, so she said she'll take care of him and I exchange he can provide extra security and earn a paycheck. She slips me his pay every Sunday when I drop by for dinner. Sunday dinners are a family thing, right? Maybe I got that from TV, but we're making it work for us. We've had three so far.

My lab partner is absent again today, but that's quite alright. For Advanced Anatomy, this class is kind of basic for me. It's cool to find out how all of the systems and everything interconnect and work together from a textbook standpoint, but the dissection and everything that the rest of the class gets excited about is just kind of blah for me. I mean, it's difficult to get excited about the inner workings of a mouse or toad or octopus when you've had the opportunity to watch someone digging around inside your own body... although the octopus was kinda cool. Tentacles are just weirdly interesting to me for some reason.

The professor doesn't like it when I try to correct him during class, so I just look out the window at the few bits of green trying to emerge in the foliage. It's been so long since I've really seen the changes of the seasons. I wish I knew as a kid that I should appreciate it more. Seeing snow for the first time again on New Year's

Eve was amazing. Starting the year off with the snow falling around us, kissing Ric, it was magic that I'll never erase from my mind.

"Mr. Sinclair," oh crap, the professor is calling for me. I stand up, wiping the tears that have managed to escape.

"Yes, sir?" I don't want to get into trouble. This is my favorite class and I can't afford to piss off this professor. He's the one I'll have as my advisor if I can get into the biology research program I want.

"You have an important phone call in the office," he says holding up a piece of paper and levels the rest of the class with a glare. "Thank you for following my rule about cell phones in the classroom."

He has this rule of if your phone goes off during class, regardless of if it's an emergency, you are marked absent for the day and lose the points associated with attendance. According to the syllabus, the only exceptions are if you inform him ahead of time that a phone call may come in, like in the event of pregnancy of a partner or if you know someone is in the hospital or in a surgery... and even then only texts are allowed. The syllabus has the administration office's number and specific instructions for us to inform all of our loved ones to call there if the emergency happens during his class time.

"Your absence shall be excused and you can just take your things with you. Send me an email if you need assistance with anything from today's lesson." At that, he dismisses me as if I don't exist. That's one of the reasons I like this prof dude. He's no nonsense. I always know where I stand with him. He's not fake friendly. He's a grumpy jerk to everyone, but at least he's fair.

I snatch up my bag and run to the administration building. I don't have a cell phone anymore, much to Bennet and Gramp's frustration. I don't really see a point. The only people I talk to or want to talk to can reach me without a phone. Why does anyone need to call me? I'm more curious than worried about this mysterious caller. I mean, who really knows that I'm still attending classes right now?

After almost wiping out on the freshly waxed floor taking the last turn through the doorway, I lean against the counter to catch my breath. The kind grandma looking lady just smiles at me and hands me a bottle of water from under her desk. Maybe I should see how she feels about vampires?

"Ethan Sinclair, I take it?" she asks me, holding up the phone. Maybe I should also learn her name...

I gulp down some water and nod before reaching for the handset. "Hello? This is Ethan."

"Mr. Sinclair, you are listed as one of the emergency contacts for one Jack Jameson, correct?" says a very proper voice on the other end. I think it's a guy, but I'm not too sure over the phone.

Oh, shit. What happened to Jack?

Where's Ric? Where's Connor? Seb? Bastien? Max?

What happened to Daddy? He should be the first one called...

"Yes! I'm his brother-in-law, well almost... maybe... I don't know... What's wrong with the kid?" I am rambling and spiraling. I need to calm down.

"He's fine. Just shaken up," says the voice on the other side. "We were told to call you."

I'm not enough of an adult to handle being someone's emergency contact. They need to get an adultier adult. But it's Jackie... and he's asking for me... and I was a major douche running out on him...

"Where is he?" I sigh into the phone. I can at least get him back home and it will give me enough time to explain things to him a bit. He needs to know I'm not ever abandoning him. I just needed to get away from the pack for a while. I thought he'd understand after my letter to him, but downside to snail mail is I don't even know if he got it.

"We'll be waiting for you at the hospital. Ask for Felix," the voice tells me. "We have some questions for you before you can get to see Jack."

Handing the phone back to the nice grandma lady, I thank her and turn to run out of the room. I slip again on the floor and almost faceplant. I'm lucky to have the reflexes I do as a wolf.

"Damn fools," I hear her mumble behind me. "I told them they need to put a rug down before someone falls and breaks their neck."

I almost chuckle, but then I remember Jack is waiting for me. Why is he at the hospital? How would he be there if no one took him? I need to call Ric, but I don't have a phone. I almost turn back to the office, but I've wasted enough time. I could reach out my way, but I'm not ready to let him back into my head...

Actually, that hasn't been all that reliable lately. I've tried to reach out to Max only to get static back sometimes. I thought my broadcasting issues were just stress last month, but all of my control with my gift seems to get worse as time goes on. That and my appetite has really been off. Maybe it's just the stress of missing my Daddy, but even coffee doesn't taste right anymore...

Can wolves get sick? Can vampires? Did the lab do something to me, like a slow acting poison that I need to regularly receive an antidote or it slowly kills me as a security measure?

Getting back to my dorm in under thirty seconds... yeah I know I should hide my speed but it's Jackie... I throw some gym clothes in my backpack and take out my books. I don't want it to be weird for me to be walking around with just clothes in my bag.

On my way out the door, something catches my eye... the letter opener I stole from Gramp's office. It was in my backpack when I grabbed my school stuff and wallet from the Jameson house. I don't really think I'll need it, but I toss it in the bag as well. The silver shouldn't set off the metal detectors at the hospital... I don't think anyways. If it does, I'll say I forgot it was in there and just swipe it back when they aren't looking.

As soon as I'm hidden by the trees, I strip and shift. Grabbing my pack in my teeth, I run as fast as I can to the hospital. I really don't have any good memories with the place and even less with doctors, but this is for Jack. He's an eight-year-old kid and scared and he asked for me. Right? I mean, that's the only way they'd call me and not anyone else... but why is he there alone?

Unless someone is using this as a trap to force me to come back. Ric wouldn't do that, would he? He wouldn't make me think Jackie's hurt just to get me back.

No. Not a chance.

If he was going to do that, he'd have me coming home, not to the hospital. This has to be legit, but now I'm worried for Daddy and Connie, too.

Connor's been talking to me on Max's phone. He sometimes comes to the coffee shop to sit with me when we can set it up. He sits and talks while I work on my schoolwork. Since Max sees me most days, it works out for all of us.

Pulling on the shoes I packed, I make my way through the parking lot. Stopping beside my favorite bright blue clunker, I smile and pat it on the roof. I don't know who this car belongs to, but it's comforting to know that no matter what, this person seems to always be around. The smell coming from the car is somehow relaxing, like an old blanket that I forgot I had...

It's in the back of my mind and I just can't reach it, but my concentration is shattered when I hear a shout ahead of me.

"Get the fuck off my car!" A very irate beta wolf is heading towards me. He looks like he hasn't slept in days and like he's about to fall over. He looks like... wait... I KNOW HIM!

"Shaun?" I ask, hardly able to contain my excitement. I'm bouncing on my feet. I know it's him!

He freezes and looks at me like he's seen a ghost.

"ETHAN?!"

We collide in a hug, almost crashing onto the hood of what I know now is his car. This was my only friend through so many years of bullying. He held me, hid me, saved me so many times. I was so angry that his family was going to move him so far away. It was supposed to happen after the school year, but I never got to finish the school year, so I have no clue when they left the Jameson pack.

"Did you end up moving away?" I ask him when we separate.

He laughs and wipes the moisture from his face. We're both crying, but I'm pretty sure they're all happy tears.

"My best friend comes back from the dead and the first thing you can think to ask is if my family moved for my dad's job like we planned?" He doubles over to try and catch his breath...

When he looks up to see my pout, he laughs even harder. It wasn't that funny.

"Sorry. I didn't know where you were and couldn't find any information or I would have found you sooner," I tell him sincerely. "I looked up everything I could, but there wasn't a record of when you left the pack or where you went. I asked around, but not many people are left that know who you are..." At that he stops laughing and gives me a funny look.

"What do you mean you couldn't find me?" he asks. He's actually angry now. "I wrote to Connor and the Alpha every single year on your birthday asking if they'd found you yet. I never believed you were dead. I NEVER gave up..."

Shaun's crying for real now. Oh, shit, now I am too. My best friend never stopped looking for me but all the grownups did. They all made him cry. I was right to run away. They don't care...

Wait... I almost forgot the reason I'm here... Jack. The grownups aren't here for him, but I am.

"Shaun, I really want to talk some more," I start walking backwards toward the hospital entrance, "but I gotta go see this Felix guy about Jackie. I gotta get him back home first."

I turn around to walk the correct way, but Shaun grabs my shoulder and spins me around. "Who?"

"Felix?" I say. "They called me and said Jack was here and I needed to answer some questions and they'd let me take him home."

Shaun is shaking his head at me and dragging me back toward his car. When we get there, he uses his key to unlock the passenger side door and shove me inside before going around the front to get in the driver's side. Once we're inside, he locks the doors and starts the engine. It's like super duper loud, but I can guess it's a good sound by the small smile on Shaun's face.

"I have to get Jackie," I tell Shaun and reach for the handle. He leans over and grabs my hand to stop me.

"He's not here," Shaun says. "Any time a supe of any flavor is brought in, all of the supernaturals on staff get an alert. Even with the kids."

He's giving me a look. I can't make sense of what he's saying.

"There was no alert, Ethan," he tells me. "Jack is not in the hospital. Even if a call came from here, no one called you to get Jack. Think about it... like really think about what was said."

I try to remember exactly what was said in the phone call. Did they actually ever say Jack was here? They asked if I was his emergency contact. I said yes. I asked how he was. They said fine. They said to come and ask for Felix and I had to answer questions before I could see Jack.

Fuck.

He was never here. I was tricked and if it wasn't for Shaun, I'd have been taken by someone... yet again. I can feel the rage building up inside me. What in the fuck is wrong with these people?

"Do I have a fucking glowing neon sign above my head that says prime kidnapping material or something?!" I shout.

Shaun spitting water all over the dash reminds me that I'm not alone in the car. I grab the other shirt out of my bag and try to wipe up the water while he is attempting to stop his coughing fit.

"Why the fuck do you think you're being kidnapped?" he asks me. "I'm not kidnapping you! I'm making sure those weirdo fae hanging around don't bother us while you find out what's going on with the Alpha's son."

"I wasn't saying you were... wait... son? Jack is Ric's brother," I tell him.

"Ric is the Alpha, as in Alaric?" he asks me. At my nod, he explains.

"When my family dipped out, Richard was Alpha and Jack was just born," he says. "I only recently moved to the area about seven or eight months ago but refused to join either pack. The Jameson pack were shit people and the Heartstones are just like their namesake. Neither wanted to listen to me when I was looking for someone to help me find you. None of the packs cared about stories from a little grieving boy who in their eyes just couldn't accept his friend died. The only one that listened was this vampire who was maybe a year or two older than us. I never found out what happened to him."

Well now this just got a bit more awkward. I squirm in my seat at his obvious anger towards pretty much everyone connected to me, everyone I love. I mean yeah, they were wrong back then and if they had listened to him, I might have been rescued sooner, but I've mostly hashed this all out with them... ok kind of... Alright, not really but they're still my family and I love them. I'm going with the ignore it and it will go away method of hashing it all out...

"You should probably know I wasn't born to the Sinclairs," I tell him. I know it's kind of left field when he gives me his WTF look. Huh, it's still the same look, except he's got stubble now.

"My bio mom was Mrs. Sinclair's half-sister and that's why they were put in charge of me. My bio dad didn't even know I existed until about a month ago."

He waves his hand in a gesture that universally signals to continue. I feel like giggling at how happy I am that he is still the same person I remember.

"Bio dad turns out is Alpha Heartstone."

The look on his face is priceless while I let it sink in. I kinda wonder what he said to my dad when he was a kid to make him get that look... Oh then he's really not going to like this next part.

"As for the Jameson pack..." Shaun looks like he's going to be sick. I let out a stress giggle. "Alpha Alaric is my fated mate and I'm an omega and we kinda killed off most of the old pack..."

Shaun cranks down his window to let in some fresh icy air. Yeah, he's going to be sick... maybe.

Before I can ask him if he's ok, he whips his gaze to the hospital doors and sniffs the air. There are two people standing in the doorway looking around. The woman looks a bit familiar, but I don't get a chance to place her before Shaun has floored it and we're racing away from the hospital. I scramble to try to get the seatbelt fastened and he just chuckles.

"Sorry E-man. Belt's busted on that side." He takes corners like a maniac and I love it.

"What kind of a car is this anyways?" I ask him. I know it's older than both of us. It's pretty beat up and ragged looking but I like the rumble of it. It feels powerful.

"This baby is a 1967 Chevy Impala, just like Baby," he tells me like he's a proud papa. I have no clue who or what Baby is, but it must be a good thing. He looks over at me in surprise.

"Baby? Supernatural? The television show..." he prompts me to try and get a reaction. I'm still clueless.

"Sammy, Dean, Cas, Crowley, Bobby, Rowena... none of it ringing a bell?"

I shake my head and giggle as he takes another hard turn. We're heading into the woods of the neutral territory towards where I found my cave if you'd go by road.

"Dude, that's it," he says as he finally slows the car to normal speeds. "We are so doing a marathon tonight. You can stay over, right? Don't have to check in or anything?"

I think about it and decide that yeah I can stay at my friend's house. If those fae people or whoever are looking for me, they can come to school to find me. They know I'm enrolled. That way, they can deal with my dad when he starts asking why they're looking for me. And then they can deal with Ric when he finds out they used Jackie to lure me to the hospital.

"Who knows where you live?" I ask him because... safety and all that.

"Just my folks," he tells me trying to hold back a sneer. I'm sure I'll get the story on that later on. "You don't have to worry about anyone finding you here and the fae can't track cars older than the 1990's. There's too much good old fashioned American steel in the bones of the car for the fae to be comfortable with them or get a read on them. Only the hybrids or the rare gremlins can handle even being inside one for longer than ten minutes. Their magic just bounces off as long as the windows are shut tight."

He pats the dash as he says this before pulling onto a trail that

I wouldn't have seen had we not actually turned onto it. He laughs at my surprise and pulls us up at a quaint cabin nestled against the side of the mountain. There's a rock shelf above it so you wouldn't see it from above and the trees block it completely from the view of the road.

"You live in a freaking secret lair!" I turn to him with glee. This was always our goal. We'd escape from our tormentors and live in our secret lair, close enough to inflict damage but far enough and hidden enough to not have to face them.

He barks out a sudden laugh while climbing out of the car on his side. I scramble to catch up to him on the porch.

"I forgot all about that," he tells me, opening the door for me to go in first. "It wasn't the intention upon finding the place, but it definitely fits... and we can pick up where we left off."

I follow his lead and throw my coat on the back of a chair in the dining nook and catch the beer he throws in my direction. I didn't really care for the beer Ric likes, but this looks like a different kind so I'll at least try it to be polite. My face must show my distaste because Shaun plucks the beer from my hand and replaces it with a Sprite.

"I keep pixie stix in the house too," he tells me with a wink. "Now let's watch some hotties face off against some of the worst caricatures of our people ever created."

I laugh as he leads me to his beat up couch with mismatched cushions. This right here is exactly where my life should have taken me without all of those detours. I belong in this cabin, with Shaun as my roommate, watching tv shows that make us laugh and groan and lust after humans that we'll never meet.

20

Unburied

Ric

"Is Jack alright?" I ask the teacher on the phone. I had just arrived at Alpha Heartstone's house when my phone rang. I answer it as I get out of the car. There is no reason for his teacher to be calling me during school hours unless it's an emergency.

"He's fine physically, but very shaken," he tells me. "Your warriors chased them off but weren't able to identify the scent of the person who approached Jack on the playground."

I'm so angry right now that someone was able to get that close to Jack to begin with. What the hell were the Things doing that they were distracted? First Ethan, now Jack. Seb is really pushing it with me and his failures lately.

"Your warriors couldn't place the scent, Alpha," Mr. Morrison repeats. "But I can. I spent my undergrad years in certain areas of Atlanta if you can understand my meaning."

Shit...

"Judging by the growl I can hear, I see you understand," he

says. "Rest assured, I am taking measures to ring the playground and any other area the children frequent in the school with iron. My classroom is already warded and protected against their kind."

What in the hell has this elementary school teacher been through that he's this paranoid about the fae? I really am failing as an Alpha if one of the teachers has this much fear for our pups and I wasn't aware of it.

"You can come get Jack if you wish, but I would recommend he stay here at the school until they are truly gone from the area," Mr. Morrison suggests. "In fact, we can make it a community event for a lock-in and do food and games and make a night of it as to not spook the parents, if you'd like... just in case Jack was just a case of opportunity and they just want any child and not specifically him."

This man is kind of great and I don't know how I've overlooked having someone like him in my pack. I remember him saying his college roommate was from our pack originally, but he never went into details. I never asked. I just saw that he had a clean record and his graduate degree in elementary education.

"Good idea," I tell him. "Have Seb make the rounds and calls to the parents and others in the community. Keep Bastien with Jack at all times. I'll try to get back there as soon as possible, but it may not be tonight or even for a few days."

"Of course, Alpha. I can also give Jack a talisman until you return, for your peace of mind," he responds before disconnecting. I am going to have to set up a meeting with some more of my pack to find out just what everyone's strengths are. I am severely under-utilizing my people.

"Yes, you are," says Edward from behind me.

I jump about ten feet in the air and would have destroyed my phone had the vampire not caught it before it made contact with the concrete of the walkway.

"How long were you listening?" I gasp out, trying to get my heartbeat to stay inside my body.

"Long enough to know we have a much bigger issue that I feared coming into this meeting."

I follow him into the house, only now noticing Bennet had been watching from the doorway. My father would be rolling over in his grave at seeing my spectacular failures right now. I can't seem to get anything right. I should have never been Alpha yet. Why did they have to go off the road that night?

Before we reach the lounge, Edward grabs my wrist in a vice grip and calls back to Alpha Heartstone, "Borrowing your office, Bennet!"

Next second, literally, he pushes me toward a chair and locks the door, closing us in the room together. This is like my worst nightmare, being trapped with a vampire. But this is Ethan's grandfather.

That makes it worse my wolf pipes up. *Can't hurt mate's family. Can't defend.*

Well, I had been controlling my anxiety, but thanks to my wolf's helpful contribution, now I can't help but think about the pain I'm about to suffer.

"Calm yourself and your damn mongrel beast," Edward growls as he pours himself a glass of whiskey from the decanter in the corner. He holds an empty glass towards me and I shake my head to decline.

"If you're going up against the fae, you need to learn the rules, boy."

He fills the glass with water and thrusts it into my hand.

"Laws of hospitality," he says as he takes a sip. "They cannot harm you if they offer you food, drink, or comfort and you willingly accept."

OK so this is a lesson... I raise the glass to my lips and at his arched brow, I hesitate before drinking.

"Very good," he says with a grin. "You must make them swear that the sustenance you are offered comes with no strings attached and you will not be beholden now or in the future for consuming what is offered."

"This is very complicated for a glass of water," I mumble trying to make sense why this is all necessary.

Edward snatches the water from my hand and pushes me back into the chair hard enough to almost topple it.

"If you don't want to lose your mate, your brother, or your pack to the fae, you need to pay the fuck attention and do as I say!"

My wolf bristles at the attack, but I subdue him. Edward might be a vampire, but he's Ethan's kin. He cares about Ethan. He's only doing this for him. Edward doesn't give two shits about me. He might care about Jack because that boy is pure happiness, but me and my pack are nothing to him.

I guess he can tell I'm sincere because he brings me the water again and asks, "What do you say before you eat or drink anything?"

"Do you swear that eating or drinking what is offered won't make me your prisoner?" I think that is the gist of it.

The vampire shakes his head. "No. It's beholden or in your debt. Can they take you prisoner? Sure, but that is temporary and against the laws of hospitality to cause you harm under their roof. You need to avoid debts. Someone in your pack or family didn't follow the rules and that's why we're here."

"It was Alpha Dick," says Max's voice from somewhere on the far side of the room. Both Edward and I jump at his voice. My pulse is getting a workout today, but I'm kind of impressed that he made the vampire jump.

He pokes his head up from the other side of the small couch in what I assume is a reading nook at the side of the office. I didn't even smell him in here.

"You don't notice a lot, Bossman," he tells me with a yawn as he stretches out before grabbing the other chair and turning it to face us.

"What was my father?" I ask him. I long ago stopped correcting him calling my father that. I figured if I stopped calling attention to it, he would stop. He didn't.

"He's the one who got into debt with a fae," he tells us, looking perfectly at ease. "He got stuck in a debt and found a way to repay it, only to get double crossed by dear old unfortunate Carl..."

Edward sucks in a breath in surprise. Obviously, he knows what is going on. I wish someone would fill me in. If my father promised my little brother to the fae, war is the least of their concern.

"Relax, boy," Edward says. "It is not your brother that Richard promised them. We have a way to fix this now that I know the situation. My thinking is correct, isn't it Maximillian?"

"I hate that name," Max grumbles before responding, "Yeah you're right if you are thinking that Dick agreed to give them Ethan in return for wiping his debt and then got screwed over royally when Carl stole Ethan out from under him."

My wolf roars out his displeasure at hearing this accusation. It's blasphemy! I jump from my chair and begin pacing the room. There's no way. I mean I thought he genuinely believed Ethan was dead... Maybe he did. But then again, if this is true, the man I looked up to so much was a monster.

What Alpha could sell one of the pups of his pack to the fae? Why would the fae even want a pup? And how in the hell did he get stuck in a deal with a fae to begin with???

"Max, may I share your memories with your Alpha so that we do not waste any more time?" Edward asks. I can barely hear him.

21

Unburied

Max

Approximately Ten Years Ago

I should have never forgotten my workbook. The options now are to grab it and risk being seen by her or go to school without my work done again and get detention. I don't mind detention so much, but I'm bordering on suspension now. I can't afford to be trapped here with her for days on end. I need school to be able to remember why living is important.

Sneaking in is more difficult than usual since she apparently threw a bottle at someone after I left this morning. I didn't think she'd have clients this early. I have to be extra careful. Now, where did I leave the workbook?

There it is! I can see it on the end table.

Houston, we have a problem... the Alpha is here and ew, they're just getting started. I can't get my workbook without them seeing me. I need to hide and wait for them to go to the room... I hope they go to her room.

I don't want to think about my mother and the Alpha getting it on where I sleep.

I manage to squeeze into the pantry only because the damn thing is always empty. There's no point in me stocking it because she'll just leave everything open to rot in her drug induced hazes... or throw it at my head. But the empty shelves work in my favor since my last growth spurt. I need the extra room for my shoulders now. Sixteen hit really hard with the hormones and the height. My shoulders are starting to get wider, but luckily malnourishment keeps a guy trim.

I barely control the sound of my surprise and the thump of my head on a shelf when the front door crashes open. Who the fuck did she piss off now? She can't find out I'm here or she'll try to use me as a bargaining chip again. I'm bigger now, but I'm still not full grown and I haven't found a decent replacement for the knife I gave to Ethan yet. It's not that easy to find a good blade when you're underage and most of her clients these days don't carry blades.

"Hello, Alpha," says a voice that's almost musical. I can't tell if it's a man or a woman. All I know is that I feel chills run down my spine at the sound of it. I don't trust whoever this is that is talking. I'm absolutely certain I don't want them to know I am here.

I can hear a scuffle and I'm too afraid to see what it is. I'm making myself as small as possible.

"Woman, you should offer refreshments to your guests, don't you know that?" says another voice. This one is more masculine, but less terrifying. Oh, shit. There's nothing in the house. If she opens the pantry, they'll see me. I can't let them see me. I know it in my gut. They can't know I'm here.

"I got water or rot gut," my mother manages to slur out in their direction. She is so fucking high she doesn't even care that there are strangers threatening her Alpha in her home. "Maybe some saltines if the pest hasn't eaten them."

"Are you offering us refreshments or just listing things?" the first voice asks.

"You can have whatever you want from my house. You find it, it's yours," she says with a bit more oomph this time. "Damn faries," I hear her mumble under her breath as I hear footsteps coming towards the kitchen.

It's a good thing the fae don't have our hearing or else she might have started a freaking war with that comment. Wait... she said anything from her house... that can apply to me. Shit.

Please don't find me. Please don't find me. They're in the kitchen now. I can see them through the crack in the door from when she fell against it a while back. They're beautiful... almost too much. Ain't nothing in this world that don't got some ugly in it. I remember my grandmother saying that before she passed when I was little.

They each snag juice boxes from the back of the fridge. Shit, I thought I hid those better. I got them for Ethan for when he comes over and I need to clean him up. It still happens from time to time and I don't want him getting sick from touching her stuff.

The man, I think he's a man anyways, stops and smells the air right in front of the pantry door. I hold my breath and do my best not to move a muscle. The fae want children according to the legends. Even though I'm almost seventeen and a man by wolf standards, I'm pretty sure the fae go by the age of the land in their judgments.

"What is it?" the first voice asks the other one.

"I think I smell a child, but I can't tell over all of... this," he says indicating to the rest of the room.

"I don't think we would want a child from here," the first voice indicates. "Although, I'm tempted to rescue the child to save them from that waste of a woman out there."

I finally let out my breath as they leave the kitchen. The Alpha is crying and begging but I can't really understand what he's saying. I hear a slap and it's silent.

"You brought them into my home, so you will do what is needed for them to get the fuck out!" my mom screams. She slapped her Alpha? She could die for that...

"Fulfill the debt you incurred, Richard son of Alistair," the first voice tells him. *"Your son or you. It's your choice."*

What the fuck?

"He is my heir!" the Alpha cries out. *"I cannot leave the pack without an heir! Plus, he's too old for you to really take in. You need someone young and flexible and already subdued, right?"*

"You promised a first-born son of an Alpha!" the second voice booms out. It shakes the house and I think I've just pissed myself.

"And you shall have one," the Alpha says seemingly more confident. *"The boy I will give you is the firstborn of an Alpha, but he has no blood family to claim or protect him. He also looks to present toward being an omega."*

Who the fuck can he be talking about? We don't have any other Alpha's children in the pack. The closest any of us come to another alpha is Connor and myself. We're alphas, but not of Alpha blood. And as for omegas, our pack hasn't had one of those for multiple generations. I've looked it up and that's why I'm leaving as soon as I can after I turn eighteen to find one. I've known women won't ever check my box since I was little. Mom just drove home the point over the years.

"This child you speak of has no family?" the first voice asks, sounding very interested.

"None that will protect him," the Alpha says.

"Very well," says the first voice. *"When he is of age and you know for certain if he is omega or not, he will come with us and your debt will be paid in full."*

"Th- Appreciated," says the Alpha. Did the asswipe seriously just promise them a kid to wipe his debt and then almost thank a fae?!

"Oh don't count your blessings just yet," says the second voice. I can tell they're heading for the front now. *"if you fail to provide the child,*

you will pay your debt yourself. There are no other chances and no other trades. This child now belongs to us, and none can stop us from claiming him."

22

———

Unburied

Ric

Coming out of Max's memory, I'm not sure what hurts more... the fact that my father was betraying my mother or the fact that he sold Ethan to cover his own ass. From the first time Ethan mentioned that my father had something to do with him being sold, I always imagined it was for the safety of the pack or some misguided loyalty to our family. But, no... he was just a selfish prick who was more afraid of losing his heir than losing his son. After experiencing what Max felt, saw, and heard in that memory, I have no doubt my father would have given them Jack if they came calling again. But they wouldn't want Jack. They wanted the first-born. They wanted me.

Instead, they were promised my mate, a boy who no one would try to protect...

Edward is just watching me as I work through my feelings. I've gone from shock to outrage to sadness to pure unadulterated rage.

He knew who Ethan's parents were. He knew who Ethan's grandfather was. He was inviting war on all of us to save his own skin...

"Yes, Alaric," Edward says as he places his hand on my shoulder. "I caught that as well, and the fae will do well to find out just how wrong your father was on that day."

Max drains his glass of whiskey that he poured at some point. "Now you understand why he always was and always will be Alpha Dick to me."

I sigh and turn toward the window. When the fuck did it get dark out? I turn in alarm to run out, but Edward stops me. "Everything is alright. My men have been keeping an eye on things."

I'm so confused. I understand why he's helping with Ethan, but why help with my pack? With Jack?

Because he is a child and pure and my grandson would never speak to me again if I ever let anything happen to that boy... and eternity is a long time to endure the silent treatment.

Wait, what? Eternity? Wolves only live about ninety or so years usually. If we're lucky, we live to be like a hundred twenty or so, but we aren't immortal.

"You figure it out yet, Bossman?" Max asks as he plops himself back onto the sofa in the nook. "Ethan's magic vampire blood makes him as long lived as his vampire line's sire line is intact or something. At least that's what these books say."

My warrior is drunk, but the look on Edward's face is telling me he's not lying.

"And since Eddie here is royalty and the royals will never die out or all vamps die or something, Ethan won't ever get old and gray... right gramps?" Max waves his hand in Edward's direction.

Shit. I might not have to worry about Ethan starting a war with the vampires, but my head warrior might just accomplish it tonight.

To my surprise, the vampire laughs and nods before saying,

"Yes, *Maximillian*... my grandson has enough of my blood to not age, but the immortality actually comes from his father."

"Hold up, please," I interrupt their banter, raising my hand like I'm in a classroom. "What is this about my mate being immortal and his father? Since when is Alpha Heartstone an immortal?"

The throat clearing from the doorway makes me lose my balance as I turn. I gotta get better at this! Too many people have been able to sneak up on me these days.

"Since my great whatever grandfather on my mother's side pissed off a witch," he says to me. "Time for dinner. Lisa made stuffed peppers tonight."

Max pushes past me, almost knocking me over, in his haste to get to the dining room. Edward just looks at my face and chuckles before following. I'm in the fucking twilight zone here. What the fuck am I supposed to do now?

"Come eat, Alaric!" calls a woman's voice. That must be Lisa. I can't do anything else at this point than go eat the stuffed peppers and try not to freak out about everything I just learned.

Ethan

After Shaun fell asleep leaning on me for the third time, I sent him to bed. He insisted I could have the bed and he'd take the couch, but I'm not kicking him out of his bed the first day we reunite. That would be shitty best friend behavior. I'll wait until tomorrow... he he he.

I can hear him snoring slightly in the other room. He always managed to end up in these weird contortionist positions when he slept and it would make him start snoring. I used to have to rearrange his limbs and head to get him to stop when we were kids. When I walk past the door of his bedroom on the way to the bathroom, I can see he's still the same. His left foot is on the wall above the headboard. His right foot is under his ass. His right arm is across his neck. His left arm is under his back and yet his hand is behind his neck. His head is hanging off the side of the bed, mouth wide open to catch all the flies.

Why did he even bother with a queen size bed if he's barely even using a corner of it? I gently move him into a more normal positioning, pulling his arms to cross over his stomach and straightening his legs out. It's easier to keep his feet towards the head of the bed than try to turn him around completely, so I just drag his shoulders enough to get his head on the bed itself.

Laughing to myself, I go in his bathroom to take care of my own nightly business. The guy in the mirror isn't familiar to me at all. My eyes are dull. I look like I've lost weight. I look sick. Is this what happens when you leave a mate? Is a broken heart enough to die from? I mean, Dad said my heart has to be intact for me to not die permanently, right? But is a broken heart figurative or literal? I think I may have one.

I'm a constant tear factory these days. I really need to stop getting the waterworks every time I think about Daddy... NOT Daddy, Ric. I kinda wish I had Mr. Whiskers here, but he's doing important things with guarding Lisa and my dad and keeping an eye on Max, making sure he doesn't do anything too crazy.

In between episodes earlier, Shaun asked me if I wanted to just stay here instead of in the dorms. I mean, if someone is coming after me, I'm safer here than the dorms. Actually, not really, but everyone else is safer if I'm here. The bad men won't have to go to pack territory and risk a war and innocent bystanders won't be caught in the crossfire like Ms. Annabel was.

I'm pretty sure that's why Grandpa Eddie kept getting that icky look every time I thought about her. I think he might blame himself for that car crash. He never actually said it, but he thinks he's the one to blame. He's not, of course. But I get where he's coming from. I blame myself for other people's actions all the time. I don't think it's healthy now that I'm on the other side of it. Once I can figure out how to stop, I'll share the secret with him.

Yawning big enough to feel my jaw pop, I realize it's time to get some snoozes myself. The couch isn't super comfortable, but it is a vast improvement to the cot and the sleeping bag back in the cave. I can use some of Mr. Whisker's paychecks to get us a better couch for me to sleep on, since I can bring him back here after dinner on Sunday. It's not wasting his money if he's sleeping here too, right?

Sleep still isn't coming after I close my eyes. My wolf is all tense but can't seem to let me know why. I try every possible position I can on the couch, but nothing works. Sitting up, I reach for the remote only to jump at the most gods-awful noise from outside. I hear Shaun fall out of bed and start scrambling for something. There's a scratching like metal on metal and next thing I see is him stalking to the front door with a shotgun in hand and a crowbar tucked in the back of his pants.

"Go back to sleep, Ethan," he tells me while looking out the window from the side of the curtain. "They'll never be able to get in here. The whole place is surrounded by iron."

Did I actually fall asleep and this is some weird ass manifestation because of the fae at the hospital and the show we were watching? I slap my cheeks and pinch my arm and yep, I'm awake. Did my best friend take me to a freaking safe house against the fae?!

"And vampires and wolves that aren't blood to those welcome here," he tells me before glancing back at me. "Yeah, I heard you. Don't know why I heard you, but I did. Been hearing you in there since the parking lot, but I don't care. I'm just happy you're alive."

He's looking like he's going to have to fight off marauders and pillagers, standing sentry with the gun. What happened to the quiet kid who used brains to fight the bullies?

"He made the wrong person feel stupid," Shaun says lowering the gun. "It looks like the defenses held. They won't be back tonight."

I have so many questions, but... "Coffee first," he says to me as he walks to the kitchen counter and pops a pod of donut shop coffee into the machine. I almost tell him to make me a cup when the smell hits me. I've never run to the toilet so fast in my life. Vamp speed is good for something at least. Ugh, that Chinese last night must not have been any good or something.

"E-man, you good?" Shaun asks knocking on the door. Surprisingly, I am good now. It's like once I got away from the smell of the coffee, I was fine.

Opening the door, I smile to tell him that I'm all good, but the smell hits me again and I'm back over the toilet. Shaun runs back to the kitchen and I hear him pouring something down the drain. When he comes back to the doorway, he has a bottle of water and some peppermints.

"No peppermints," I say in horror. I back away and the shaking starts. I can't be around that smell. I can't do it.

I'm not there. I'm not there. Connie got me out. I'm not there.

I feel myself being led somewhere. It's not rough like I'm expecting. It's gentle and I feel softness underneath me. This is so much better than the cot. As I close my eyes, I feel more softness placed over my body. This is nice. This doesn't belong...

Slowly my conscious mind comes back online and I can see Shaun sitting in a folding chair by the door, reading a book. I don't know how long I was out of it this time. Did I pass out? When did I get in a bed?

"What happened?" I ask him, sitting up and swaying a little bit. Why am I dizzy?

"Well...you threw up. You remember that, right?" he asks and I nod. I remember that much.

"I went to give you some mints and you just kinda freaked out and then went catatonic on me."

Oh. At least I didn't start sucking my thumb and screaming for Mr. Whiskers this time... this is bad enough...

"I know PTSD when I see it, Ethan," he tells me. "You don't have to tell me about it, but please just let me know of any triggers you know of, like the peppermint smell, so that I can do what I can to mitigate it"

What is he talking about? What's PTSD? "You mean there's a name for my episodes?" I ask him. I'm genuinely curious now because if there's a name for it, that means I'm not a freak for having them.

"You're not a freak," he growls out. "Why doesn't Alaric have you in some kind of therapy? Or your father? PTSD is totally manageable with therapy, sometimes medication, and even the use of service animals."

"I don't do doctors," I tell him as I curl up into as small of a ball as I can. I don't want to tell him what happened. We're back to the best friends we were. I want to stay there. I don't want to be the broken omega to be pitied anymore. I'm either hated or pitied. I like being just Ethan. I don't want to stop being just Ethan.

"Don't make me tell you, please," I beg him as the tears start to fall. Damn eyes don't want to stay dry anymore. Wiping at my face, I shout to no one in particular, "Can't I go one damn day without crying anymore?!"

"Doubt it," Shaun says getting up from the chair. He looks really sad. Did I hurt him?

"I'm Sor-"

He slaps his hand over my mouth to shut me up. I raise my eyebrow in question and he laughs at me.

"Stop apologizing for things that aren't your fault," he tells me as he sits next to me on the bed. "You're not going to like what I'm going to say... any of what I'm going to say. But I need you to promise me you won't run from this house."

He sounds really serious. I can't think of anything he can say that will make me run, so I nod.

"I mean it, Ethan. If you want away from me, I'll drive you back to the dorms, but you can't go somewhere unprotected. If you aren't in this house, you have to be on pack lands. Tell me you understand and promise me."

"Does it have to be pack lands?" I ask him. I'm not ready to go home yet, but I'm mad at my father and don't want to go to his house either. The dorm is full of innocent bystanders. But there is one other place I can go that the fae shouldn't want to mess with.

"Where are you thinking?" he asks me.

"The warehouse district," I tell him.

He about falls off the bed in his surprise. I giggle at the look on his face. Man, I wish I had my phone to get a picture of this look. It would so be his contact photo in my phone.

"The vampires will kill you for trespassing!" he screeches at me. "Are you fucking insane?"

Oh yeah, I guess I never got around to sharing that little bit of my family tree with him last night.

"About that..." I run my fingers through my hair trying to figure out how to say it. "King Edward is kinda sorta my gramps so I'm kinda sorta always welcome there or in any of the vamp properties in the US..." I trail off and watch Shaun's face grow redder and redder. Did he forget to breathe?

I slap him on the shoulder and he takes a huge breath in. Yep. He forgot to breathe. I think that's the first time I've ever shocked someone into not breathing.

"OK well my news shouldn't be so bad then." He mutters. "Just promise you won't be alone in any neutral areas, ok? I'll drive you wherever you need to go."

"Promise. Cross my heart and all that jazz, although the hope to die thing apparently doesn't work with me," I say to him and he looks like he's going to question it but shakes himself out.

"That's not important right now. Item number one that you need to know is that you are pregnant," he says watching for my reaction. I don't really have one. I'm more confused than anything else. How am I pregnant when I don't have sex? Ric never pushed for it and I never wanted to... well mostly never. We've tried some things that wouldn't result in pregnancy, but his dick hasn't gone in down there since my heat...

My heat in January... I don't remember it and Ric wasn't there before or after, but I didn't come to myself in any sort of pain. It's supposed to be extremely painful and difficult to recover from if you don't have sex during it, right? I wasn't in pain. We had sex... and I'm... and he's... and now...

Here come the waterworks again. What am I supposed to do now? I can't be a single omega with a kid going to college. And oh. My. Gods... what if it's a son? First born son and the curse thingy dad was talking about? I can't be a papa yet. I'm not ready. I'm not old enough. I'm not good enough.

"Breathe, Ethan." I can hear him repeating it over and over while he runs his hand up and down my back. There's a huge wet spot on his shoulder. How long was I crying on him?

"You're ok. You and the babes are healthy," he says to me softly. I curl into him for a moment before what he just said registers...

"BABES?" I shout sitting up way too fast and having to lean back against the headboard.

"Yeah," he says sheepishly grabbing the back of his neck. "It's kind of my specialty..."

I stare at him like he's going to have an evil clown or something pop out of the closet to eat me and my unborn children. What the fuck isn't he saying? What is wrong with my babies?

"I'm an OB resident at the hospital, Ethan."

He looks like a bomb is going to go off at any second. I'm not following what the tension is all about.

"And why do you look like you're waiting for me to explode?" I ask him.

He looks up and I can see the confusion on his face.

"You said you don't do doctors. You're pretty adamant that you hate them all, right?"

I nod, still not following.

"E-man, I'm an obstetrician. I'm a baby doc," he tells me and it clicks. My best friend is the thing I fear and despise the most in the world. I can't breathe. The world is going gray. He's touching me, laying me down on my side. I don't want him to touch me. Never again. No more doctors. No more... please no more. I'll be good. I promise. No more doctors, please...

I feel the hands pull away from me like I finally have the power to force them away. I wish it was truth. The voice on the phone probably ordered them away. I kinda hear someone crying nearby. I hope they haven't found someone new again. It's so much harder to pretend I'm somewhere else when they start screaming. It takes a while to ignore the new screams, and longer for them to stop.

23

Unburied

Ric

Dinner was amazing, but what shocked me the most was seeing Mr. Whiskers right there at the table and everyone acting like this was normal. I half expected my boy to walk in the door and sit down to eat with us, but unfortunately, the dinner was mostly uneventful.

After we all ate, Alpha Heartstone led us all back to his office for more discussion. We've been in here for about an hour just going over all of the different things the deal with the fae actually involved and how we can use their own words against them. So far, we haven't found a loophole to fully nullify their claim to Ethan if they choose to push it.

If we can't find a way, then we all have to prepare for war. None of us want to give him up to the fae... especially the ones from Max's memory. The way things were worded, it sounds like they wanted him for a slave. The way my father worded things, it sounds like he was thinking sex slave. I don't bother to suppress the growl from my wolf and at the room's reaction, I must have had some really bad timing.

"You disapprove of the plan, Alaric?" Edward asks me, raising his eyebrow. Huh, so that's where Ethan's eyebrows come from.

The Alpha clears his throat to get my attention. Apparently, I am zoning out way too much. Before I can start apologizing or thinking up an excuse other than being stuck on hating my father, Bennet's phone starts to ring.

"Yes, Jasmine?" he answers. As he listens, his face grows darker, his eyes harder. "Why wasn't I informed when he got a call?!"

We all sit up a bit straighter and don't even hide that we're trying to listen in. The person on the other end of the call is in a panic.

"He came back to the dorm after the call, so no alert was triggered," the woman says. "It wasn't until the RA did bed checks that anyone noticed he was gone."

My brain is a little slow lately, but I got the gist. Ethan isn't where he's supposed to be and it's almost three in the morning and no one knows how long he's been gone... Thinking about the incident with Jack, I don't hesitate to ask.

"Can the fae get onto your pack territory and have access to the university?"

"Like they had access to your elementary school?" Bennet growls back at me. I hold back my snarl. Us fighting does nothing to help Ethan if the fae got to him.

"Alaric is right," Edward pipes up before Bennet gets to the point of throwing blows. "Fighting amongst ourselves doesn't help the boy. Now, answer his question, Mongrel!"

At the insult, every wolf in the room starts to growl and stare at the vampire. Three of the four strongest wolves in the area are in the room and he looks like we are gnats to him.

"Could those nature freaks have gotten to my grandson or not?!" he demands of Bennet.

Without meaning to, we're all on our knees in front of the vampire. This is the true power behind the royals. If he wanted to, Edward could kill us all without ever lifting his pinky. In fact, he has the reputation of doing just that when angered. Ethan's love for us is what is saving us.

"The university is public space, so yes they could get to the academic and administration buildings," Bennet says after a moment trying to fight the compulsion. "But the dorms are not public space, especially the one I had my son placed in. The beams for not only the outer shell of the building but the studs for each room as well are made of raw steel. The iron was unprocessed as much as possible."

"You knew the fae were a threat?" Max asks rising from his knees to stare at the Alpha. "You knew and didn't prepare us?"

I've never seen Max get angry with anyone before. He never loses his temper, but he's vibrating with rage as he steps up next to the vampire and stares down at the Alpha who is still on his knees.

"You told me he was safe!" Max yells at the man on the floor in front of him. "You told me I should stay behind and help with the research to break the deal… but thanks to you, Ethan is…"

I rush to my feet to catch my warrior before he collapses into sobs. He's saying something, but I can't really hear it through his tears and heaving breaths.

He can't get taken again. He's the reason I'm alive. He saved me. I have to save him. I have to protect him. He can't be gone again. I can't live if he's gone. I won't…

I feel myself pulled from Max's mind and meet Edward's eyes. There's a deeper connection between Max and Ethan than any of us know about. My warrior is too secretive, even for a mind reader like the vampire. And my bluebird doesn't share what isn't immediately running through his mind. I only know most of what I know because of the memory bleeds when he's asleep.

"You see his memories?" Edward asks me as I manage to get Max laid down on the sofa. "How long has that been happening?"

I stop and think about it. I want to say as soon as we met as adults, but I think it has more to do with the fact that I claimed him, thinking I was saving his life, not knowing he would come back. The half claim created a bond that the memories bled through consistently before we completed the claim.

"It was a temporary thing as far as him doing it unconsciously," I tell him. "Things... happened and it created a half claiming between us for a while."

I have the feeling Edward was following my thoughts, but I made sure to voice it out loud for Bennet's sake. He is still kneeling with his head down. He hasn't moved at all.

"He bonded before the completed claim," Edward says under his breath. "You might be able to find him through the bond if he allows it." He looks at me with such hope.

If my boy allows it, I can find him. If he allows it... He already said goodbye. Why would he want ME to find him?

"Get your head out of your ass and find my son!" snarls Bennet from the floor. He hasn't gotten up, but his raised head shows the red eyes he was trying to hide. "I fucked up. You fucked up. We all fucked up. But you have the chance to fix it, so fucking do it already!"

Swallowing my anger and pride at the way the other Alpha spoke to me, I look inside myself to try and find the connection to my boy. I can feel a slight tug back when I pull at something, but he still won't answer when I try to reach out to him. In fact, I get thrown physically to the floor when I try to talk to him.

24

Unburied

Ric

"That's different," the vampire says as he reaches out to help me stand back up. "I've never seen a psychic rejection become a physical attack before."

"Is it the fae's doing?" Bennet asks, finally getting his feet back under him. "Did they stop Ric?"

Edward looks like he's almost tasting the air like a snake. "No," he says with a bit of surprise. "He's with a wolf who is a witch, or part witch. That wolf is protecting him…"

A wolf witch hybrid? I don't have one in my pack and from the look on the other Alpha's face, neither does he. Where the fuck is my bluebird and where in the hell did he meet this werewitch? And yes I just made up the word because it will take too much time to say all the hybrid designations all the time.

Edward cracks a smile but doesn't break his concentration for a few minutes. We're waiting for something, but he frowns and looks at me directly.

"Ethan is not injured," he says looking at me sadly. What is he not telling me?

"The wolf says his name is one you'd know if you truly know your mate and until we know his name, we won't know where Ethan is."

Bennet gets up and storms from the room, slamming the door open hard enough to crack the plaster. As the door swings back to shut, we can see the steel beams in the walls here.

"Why does he fear the fae so much?" I ask to no one in particular.

"Because his great whatever grandmother was one," says Lisa pushing the door back open to bring in a tea tray with a fresh pot and some cookies. "The fae don't like reminders in the world that they aren't pure. They don't like any fae blood not under their control."

This woman is amazing. She reminds me of Mom so much. She loved Ethan so much. I really wish she was still here for his sake, and Jack's. Jackie really needs a mom in his life...

The silence in the room is disrupted when Max's phone starts ringing. Lifting it to his face, he hits the ignore button and covers his eyes. The phone rings again, and he hits ignore again. The third time it rings, I grab it from him before he can ignore it. The screen is blank. It doesn't even say unknown or anonymous. This is magic that can affect technology. This is a modern witch calling us.

"You remembered my name?" says a voice on the other end when I answer and put it on speaker. I look at Max. I'm completely clueless as to who this could possibly be. I don't recognize the voice at all.

"You're the brat who tried to help him back then, aren't you?" Max asks, not lifting his arm from across his eyes. "Shaun, right?"

"I never thought you were as dumb as you looked, Maxi-pad"

says the voice coming out of the speaker. And now I remember him. He was a quiet kid, but he stuck to Ethan like glue. The two were inseparable most of the time...

You'd have to ask Shaun who they were. I never saw them...

Ethan's recollection of the bike incident flies into my head at that moment.

"Who were the kids on the bikes," I ask to the phone. Edward gives me a look like I'm insane. He doesn't understand that I need to know that we took care of all of the threats to Ethan in my pack. If he names someone who I spared, they will know pain that even my little psycho can't dish out.

"Bikes?"

"The bikes, when Ethan busted his rim, around his eighth birthday or so..." I prompt him because, yeah it is kinda out of left field.

"Oh that time? Yeah it was Timmy Donovan, Justin O'Keefe, and Sidney Black that ran him off the trail. I tried to catch up in time to stop them, but my bike popped the chain. I got there as quick as I could once I saw them riding away..."

Why is it that I'm only finding out now that everyone else was protecting Ethan while I thought it was enough to sneak him some candy? I am a shit person.

"You aren't a bad person for having a good life, douchebag. You're not even a bad person for not listening to a kid screaming his best friend was alive. You were so lost in grief you lost sight of everything but your own best friend...makes me wonder which Sinclair you actually wanted for your mate," comes the voice from the phone...Shaun. Ethan's best friend... the kid who sent my dad letters and emails saying Ethan was alive and we had to find him...

Oh shit...

"Yeah, you figured it out didn't you, RRRRRic?," he snarls over the line. "I told you all he wasn't dead, but no one listened. For years, I said it but none of you listened. I went looking for help to find him and NONE OF YOU LISTENED."

We're all silent in the room. Bennet had rejoined us at some point, but even he is staring at the phone in shock.

"The Jameson pack abandoned him completely, leaving the state when he was just an hour away, praying daily for someone to set him free from that place, one way or another."

I can feel the stares of everyone in the room. It's the truth. We were all grieving and the kid was making it harder. Dad kicked his family out of the pack right after the move here. Mom had just had Jack and I guess the stress just got to everyone... no... Dad didn't want his secret to get out...

"The Heartstone pack told me that they didn't meddle in death investigations and that I should get therapy to get over the death of my friend."

Bennet looks like he wants to throw up. There's no way he could have known the friend in question was his son, but at the same time he is directly responsible in his own way for Ethan remaining in that place.

"His vampire sire felt the blood song but did nothing to locate him except feel guilty and call it a dead end when his only lead drove off a cliff."

Edward's gaze snaps to the phone in my hand. Something tells me that Shaun should not know those details.

"The only person who listened and helped was a sixteen-year-old vampire who didn't want to be the next king. He jumped at the chance to help someone who really needed it... and spent over two years in that hell himself."

The look on the vampire's face can only be described as dumb-struck. There's grief and anger there, but the things that Shaun is saying suggest that the vampire that was in the lab with Ethan is also related to Edward. Could that be the vampire from the night at the warehouse?

Max looks extremely interested at this piece of news. Interested and pissed and a little sick...

"But placing the blame for what happened falls to all of us and none of us at the same time," he tells us as we are all trying to digest the bombs he's dropped on us. "The real culprit in all of the things that happened to him is Esther Sinclair, but she's dead. From her, we can move on to Richard Jameson, but again, he's dead. Then there's Carl Welling, yet again dead."

"Every person who truly wronged him is dead," Shaun says very clearly with power behind the words. "Karma and the fates will decide who has wronged him and they will mete out their punishment and their punishment shall be death."

The silence that echoes after his statement stretches on until there is a popping noise coming from the phone.

"Ok now that that's done," he says in a more chipper tone, "how do you wanna handle this fae shit going on, cuz I can keep him here and he'll be safe but I doubt he's gonna wanna stay once he wakes back up."

"Why wouldn't he want to stay?" I ask at the same time Bennet asks "How can you keep him safe?"

"Alpha Heartstone, puh-lease! I'm a witch and a wolf and a genius and I've been running from the fae pretty much since Alpha Dick kicked us out of the Jameson pack," he states like it is no big deal.

"My house is hidden by iron, steel, and oak. The cliff at the back of my house has iron ore running through the rocks and the overhang blocks the sight of my house from above. My drive is invisible due to proper terrain development and the oaks protect my home from the view of those who would do me or my guests harm. There are old rail tracks from the iron mines that run along the perimeter of my property and I may have manipulated them a bit to completely seal my property from the fae."

Edward and Bennet both look suitably impressed at what they're hearing from Shaun as far as defense against the fae.

"Oh, and don't forget I'm a witch, so spells to keep out trespassers and intruders and any beings with malicious intent and people I just don't like... you know, the usual" he adds with a chuckle.

"Sounds like the safest place for him," Max says sitting up, finally looking like his old self again. "What's the issue?"

"See, I thought he knew and I didn't know about him having PTSD and everything," Shaun starts and growls are coming from everyone in the room, not only me.

"RELAX!" Shaun hurries to say, "I'm not judging him for having PTSD. It's only natural considering what he's gone through... although the no therapy thing is something I do have an issue with but that's just because I'm a doctor myself..."

Mine and Max's growls cut off abruptly. Edward and Bennet look at us curiously. Now, it's obvious...

"I understand why you think he won't stay there with you," I say to the phone. "Would you be willing to stay somewhere else and allow Ethan to stay there with say, Max? or even Connor? I know I'm not welcome..."

"I'd let you in long before I'd ever grant access to that piece of shit Connor," he snarls back at me. I wasn't aware of any bad blood, but I look at Max and he shrugs. News to both of us it seems. "Max can come, and the vampire that helped... no others will find my house so send no one else unless you want to lose them in the woods."

I can tell he's about to hang up, but I have to ask for another favor. "Shaun? Can I get one more favor from you?"

"This is for Ethan, not for you," he says. "If it wasn't for the fact that he won't stay in this house if I'm here, I'd have let you stew in the knowledge that he was outside of the precious pack protection you guys all seem to believe is flawless."

"Ethan would want Jackie safe," I rush to say before he can hang up the phone.

"And why would Ethan want to protect this Jackie?"

"Jack is the Alpha's little bro and he's sweet and innocent and everything that Ethan should have been if the pack wasn't such shit back then," Max tells Shaun, and the rest of the room. I remember then that they've heard of Jack, but Max is the only one who has met him.

There's silence on the other end of the line for a while. I light up the screen just to make sure the call is still connected.

Shaun lets out a sigh eventually and agrees that Jack can come there too, but only if he's brought by Max or the vampire. When he disconnects the call, Max gives us all a look before he grabs his phone and leaves the room. The sound of his motorcycle revving up and tearing off down the street is the only indication we have that he's going to Ethan.

"Joshua will go as well, I'm sure," says Edward with an odd look on his face. "How trustworthy is this Shaun fellow?" he asks me pointedly.

"He'd never hurt Ethan," I tell him and can feel the truth in my bones.

"But would he trade another to save him? That is what I fear now," Edward mutters under his breath. I think he forgot about werewolf hearing...

25

Unburied

Ethan

Man, that was a weird ass dream. Talking impalas, pulling holy oil out of an ass, really hot guys doing lip syncs and karaoke... oh wait. That's right. We were watching that show. I must have fallen asleep while watching. That's the only reason that it makes sense for me to find out my best friend is the thing I am most terrified of in the universe and that I've got not just one but two buns in the oven that the G Lady can lay claim to if I fuck up and kill by accident.

Right? It's all just a dream induced by that crazy tv show. Has to be...

The smell of coffee wafts into the room from down the hall and I'm suddenly over the toilet upchucking nothing at all. I must have gotten it all out last night. So it's not a dream then.

I really am knocked up again... with two this time. And my bestest friend ever is a d-word. How in the hell do I face him? I don't want to have an episode in front of him...

Wait a second, I already did, didn't I? The peppermints thing. That's right. So he already knows I'm messed up in the head now and he knows I don't like the d-word people. How do I leave this room and go out there, knowing what I know now?

"You can come out E-man," he calls to me. "I dumped the coffee already. I made some tea instead."

Creeping around the corner, I don't notice my thumb in my mouth until he chuckles. I stand up straight and try to be cool, but it's embarrassing as fuck to have it happen like that. At least I know I can trust him, at least subconsciously, if my thumb was in my mouth in front of him. My toddler side knows who he can trust by instinct. He generally doesn't come out if he doesn't trust the people or situation around me.

"So you're a d-word? How'd that happen?" I ask him. "I mean we're both twenty-one. I thought you needed like ten years of college to do that kind of thing. Or is that just something they say to make you spend a shit ton on tuition?"

He laughs and sips his tea before explaining, "I graduated high school at fourteen doing online school. After we were kicked out of the Jameson pack, Mom and Dad moved us to Atlanta, not real-izing it was hardcore fae territory. Dad pulled some magical strings to get me into college at age fifteen and Mom forced me to stay in the dorms because they were magically protected or some-thing. I didn't understand at the time."

I'm getting the feeling that the story is not a happy one by the way his body tightens up as he continues, "I got my bachelors of science for the pre-med requirements by the time I turned sixteen. I was going to leave the area for medical school, but I kept getting rejected from every school except for the ones in Atlanta. Turns out the fae found out about me."

"Since I was just a child, but alone in the dorms, they thought I was unprotected. They tried to steal me, force me into their world, by eliminating my escape from their territory. But my roommate got a job here with the Jameson pack as a school teacher and he dragged me up here and we escaped the fae together. He stays safe in the pack and I managed to snag my internship in Charleston and residency at the hospital here. Because it's not technically a supe hospital, being in neutral land, the fae couldn't find me. As long as I stay neutral, they can't find me with the talismans and spells I use."

He's been through shit just like me... so what if he's the d-word. He is a baby d-word. He wasn't the kind that I dealt with before. Plus, this is Shaun. Shaun wouldn't do anything to hurt me, ever. Besties forever and all that stuff.

While he's staring into his teacup like it holds the secrets of the universe or something, I walk around the little table to give him a hug. I want my best friend back. Fuck it that he's a d-word. He was Shaun first and he's going to be Shaun after. I can feel his shoulders shaking, but he's making no sounds. Someone taught him to cry silently. I'm going to destroy the one who did that.

26

Ethan

The knock on the door makes me jump, but Shaun just chuckles and stands up. He doesn't seem worried about whoever just showed up at his secret lair in the middle of no man's land. I get ready to run, just in case. I didn't last this long being totally stupid, only kind of situationally stupid.

As the door opens to reveal the guests, I squeal in excitement and there's an echo from across the room. Jackie speeds into my arms for a hug and I vaguely hear Max and Shaun laughing. I don't care. Jackie's here and he's safe and it's been way too long since I've seen him. Has he grown a few inches? It's only been a little over a month!

And I'm crying again. Damnit! I was really hoping the pregnancy thing was a bad joke. I don't remember seeing anyone like this, but the movies and tv shows and everything seem to make women out to be emotional wrecks when they're pregnant so I guess it makes sense. I don't want to have to go through months of this crap.

Hold up... since omegas are unique and all, does that mean there are different rules for being pregnant as one? I look over at Shaun and Max exchanging greetings and wave to get their attention.

How long will I be knocked up? Is it different for me as an omega?

I meant to send it only to Shaun, but apparently my ability is still on the fritz cuz Max steps back into the coatrack in shock, almost toppling it and him over. Jackie looks up at me and asks, "I'm gonna be a big brother?"

Oh gods. He's too precious. I can't answer through the tears and just hold him tighter.

I don't know how long we're like that before Max gently pulls him from my arms.

"Let the kid breathe," he says to me and ruffles my hair. He leads Jack to the ugly couch and sits down with him. "You won't get anymore brothers, kiddo."

Jack looks crestfallen at that suggestion. Why did Max have to say that to him? Yeah it's true that he won't get any other brothers or sisters, but don't take that away from him. I don't know what's come over me, but next thing I know my hand stings and Max is holding the back of his head.

"What the fuck, Ethan?!"

"Don't make him sad!" I say instead of the apology I wanted to say. What the hell is wrong with me?

Shaun steps into the space between us and gently leads me to the recliner, indicating I should sit. I plop myself down and curl up as much as I can... pretty soon I won't be able to sit like this anymore with two pups inside me. I need Mr. Whiskers.

"Max?" he looks up at me, still kinda pissed. "Do you think you can get Mr. Whiskers for me?"

His whole body relaxes and he goes back to the door. I know the big lug likes me, but didn't think he'd leave again himself. He doesn't leave though. Right inside the door are three duffle bags. He reaches inside one and pulls out Mr. Whiskers and a note.

"He figured you'd need him with you so he made me sneak him away from Lisa and Bennet," Max says as he hands me both.

I don't need to ask what "he" is being referred to. Gramps and Dad have no idea the importance of Mr. Whiskers to me. They've never seen my episodes. They never saw my nightmares.

My Darling Blue,

I hope your nightmares haven't caused you problems without your hunter by your side.
Know he did his job well in your absence.
You are both welcome home whenever you're ready when this is all over, but first we need to make sure you're safe.
Know I love you, now and always.

-Daddy

It could have been minutes or hours or even days that I sat in that chair clutching my teddy and staring at that note. Time has lost its meaning for me. Shaun is keeping Jack occupied with the tv and some video game system he got. I'm still not caught up on all of that. Fake mom never let me play games and well, I wasn't exactly given leisure time in the lab.

I only notice it's turned dark outside when Max places his hand on my head. "You wanna talk about things, little dude?"

Shaun is getting dinner ready for Jack, who is sitting at the small table with some activity books... might even be his home-work... school. Shit! I missed another day!

Max sees my anxiety and makes some weird shushing noises and it kinda helps. I think it's more the juxtaposition of this big burly lug being so super sweet and gentle that helps to snap me out of the panic spiral I was starting in on.

I get up and head to the bedroom. My muscles are all crampy from sitting like that for so long and I want to stretch out and have at least a bit of privacy for our talk. I hear a radio turn on from the other room and smile. Shaun really is the bestest best friend ever.

Max closes the door behind him and pulls out the folding chair Shaun had used earlier, but I flop my preggo ass back on the bed sideways, all spread out star-fish like. It's exhausting being me these last few days. First the scare with Jackie at the hospital. Then the anti-fae security alarm. Then the oh, by the way you're preggo. Then the oh yeah, your best friend who you're alone in an isolated cabin in the woods that no one knows where it is happens to be a d-word... and now my little sunshine is going to be crushed because he's never going to have a new brother.

"First of all," Max says, making me raise my head to look at him. "He's not going to be crushed. He'll be ecstatic that he gets to be an uncle."

That makes me feel a bit better, and I raise up on my elbows so that my neck doesn't get a permanent crick in it. I kinda want to grab a pillow or twelve to get more comfortable, but I just can't reach them from where I am and fuck it I don't want to move right now.

Max chuckles as he stands and heads toward me on the bed. He lifts me up and I squeak. Well, that's embarrassing. No grown man should ever make that kind of a noise. Max can't stop laughing and almost drops me before he manages to get me sitting against the headboard with pillows behind my back. He practically falls onto the bed to sit next to me, our legs stretching down. My legs barely hit the halfway point. His are at like the three quarters mark... How does he find a bed to fit him?

"OK. Enough about me in beds," he manages to get out between bouts of laughter. "Ric would kill me if he heard this."

The smile falls from my face. I can't help it. It takes Max a second to realize it, but when he does, he just puts his arm around my shoulders and pulls me to his side. I'm not ready to talk about Daddy...Ric. I want him to be Daddy so badly, but I just know he won't want me anymore... Will he want the babies? I'm sure he'll want one of them for his heir, but maybe he'll let me keep the other one. Then again, there's a good chance I'll be a terrible papa, so it's better if he keeps them both. Babies need to be raised by their real parents.

"That is absolute bullshit," growls Max. I keep forgetting my quirk is on the fritz, so I guess he heard all of that...

"Just because someone gives birth or donates sperm, it doesn't mean they will be good parents," he snarls to the ceiling. "Just look at my ma, Ric's dad... Not everyone should be a parent, but you will be an amazing papa."

He kisses my head and rubs my shoulder, "You have enough love for these kids already that they will never know any of the fear or pain that we did..." I'm crying again, but this time it's me and not the hormones.

"But what if I'm not there?" I ask, horrified at remembering something kind of vital from my own history. "What if I don't make it?"

"I promise you, Blue, if anything happens to you and I'm still alive, those kids will still know your love and I'll protect them the way I wanted to protect you from the day we met."

As he pulls me in tighter for a hug, I'm suddenly bombarded by Max's memories. I'm not trying to see them. I don't want to see them. But my ability is so freaking haywire lately that it's like it has a mind of its own.

I see his reflection in the mirror. He's about Jackie's age. He's covered in cuts and bruises. A woman calls for him and he runs to hide. *"Come to Mama, Maximillian. There's a special lady here to meet you..."* I can feel his fear and disgust as he climbs out the window, adding another gash to his arm. *Better a bloody arm than going through that again...*

I see him staring across the pond at the other kids, about thirteen at this point. They're all talking about getting their wolves. Some of them, like Connor are showing off having their wolves by shifting. The girls in the group are all looking at him like he's prey. *He deserves the looks the spoiled little princeling. He doesn't know what it feels like. Let him find out how it feels to have that done to him and see how much he can smile then.*

Ric walks away from the group, saying something about having a headache. He comes to a stop just in front of where Max is hiding. *"I wish my wolf would be early. I'm supposed to be their leader, but I come in last as usual,"* the boy mutters under his breath. There are tears falling from his eyes, but no one across the pond would be able to tell. *I didn't know the Alpha heir could show emotion...*

I don't even realize when it happens, but instead of observing Max's memories, suddenly I'm Max and I'm seeing things through his eyes, hearing his thoughts, feeling what he felt...

I'm with all the kids from the pond. It's maybe a year or so later. "Your little brother is creeping around again," whines the whore-bitch. *She's going to end up just like Mama, flat on her back and good for nothing else.* Connor and Ric just chuckle while the rest of the group groans. *We're in the freaking Beta house. Of course, the kid will be around.* "Let's head to the diner, then" someone else suggests.

Everyone else packs up and heads out to the door, but I really gotta pee, so I ask Connor where the bathroom is.

Finishing up, I exit the room to see Mrs. Sinclair with a bloody candlestick in her hand and the little dude on the floor, trying to catch the blood from his head before it can reach the rug. She freezes for a second and then smirks as she places who I am. The kid doesn't even see me in his state. I run from the room and the house. *They can go eat burgers and fries and whatever, but I can't pretend to be happy after seeing that.*

Walking home from the library, I take a different route than usual. *Maybe this way, I can avoid seeing Mama's clients on their way in or out.* There's a commotion off to the side, but I'm not too worried. There are some seedy places around here. When I glance to my right, I do a double take. *What the fuck are kids doing in this neighborhood?* And these are the rich kids, too. If they were older, I'd think they were looking for drugs, but nah, these are elementary kids. They're beating on something. *Poor cat.*

Chasing them off is easy. I've started my growth spurt. I'm already over six foot, so I must look like a giant to the twerps. I pull my trusty switchblade out of my pocket to put the thing out of its misery, but it's not a cat. It's another kid... not just any kid. This is the Beta's kid, the little one. *What in the hell is going on with him?*

I'm crouching in the pantry, pants soaked in urine when I hear the Alpha promise a child to the fae that came to collect his debt....

27

Unburied

Ethan

"What the fuck?!" I say out loud, breaking the connection of the memories from Max. "Alpha Dick promised me to the fucking faeries?"

"How did you know?" Max asks me, trying to read my face. "I didn't say anything and I've gotten very good at blocking and reorganizing my thoughts thanks to being around your grandfather."

I look around the room, making a point to look anywhere but at him. "Well you see," I start, but I can't figure out how to tell him.

"What is going on, Ethan?" he asks holding my chin in place so that I have to look at him. I guess if I have to come clean to someone, he's the one to do it with. He doesn't judge me... usually.

"The thing is..." I start again, but this time I think I know how to say it. "I have no clue why it's happening, but I'm pretty sure my ability is on the fritz, going loco, doing its own thang, ya know? I have no control over it whatsoever right now."

"So how'd you know about Alpha Dick?"

"I kinda sorta went into your memories and got stuck going through some of them," I tell him looking at my hands in my lap. "I wanted to stop looking right away, but it wasn't until I heard what he said to the fae that I snapped out of it. I didn't mean to look! I swear I'd never violate you like that! I'm so sorry, Max!"

By the end, I'm practically in his lap hugging him. He has to forgive me. I can't lose him. Yeah, it would hurt to lose the others, but I need Max to be there for my babies. He's the only one who knows what to look out for. He's the only one who knows how to see. He knows more than me. My babies need him..

"Shhh, little dude," he whispers, rubbing circles on my back while I soak his neck with tears. "I got you. And I got the babies, too. Don't worry. I won't let anyone hurt them like we were hurt. And I mean anyone..."

The tone of his voice makes me sit up and look him in the eyes. My sniffles kind of ruin the moment, but I get what he's saying. He'll even protect them from me if it becomes necessary. A weight I didn't even know was there suddenly lifts from me and I feel like I can relax for the first time since Shaun gave me the news. I didn't know I was even worried about me hurting them or being abusive until now.

I don't mean to fall asleep but laying my head back on Max's shoulder, I let out a hiccup and a sigh and next thing I know, I'm in a memory. I'm not sure who it belongs to. I know it's not mine.

28

Unburied

Speeding through the treetops is fun. I'll have to remember to tell Ethan I gave it a try after all. Those days in the lab were miserable except for when they would pit us against each other. The stupid humans didn't realize we never showed our full potential in there. We usually found a way to work out a winner ahead of time or through whispers or, in some cases mind speak, to choreograph the fights.

Ethan was really good at telegraphing his moves. I don't think he realized we could all hear him. It's a good thing the humans weren't able to though. The boy had zero blocks in his mind. I guess he never needed them, seeing as how he ended up in here right as he came of age.

To say my uncle was upset at learning that I found him in the lab would be an understatement. He practically destroyed his house in his rage. I would like to think that some of that was for me and how I was treated in there, but I know better.

I'm just a worthless replacement, a pretty piece to dangle in front of everyone so that he can pretend he's going to step down some day. He's royalty that will live forever, why the fuck would he ever want to step down with the way the world bows down to him?

I need to slow down since I'm getting closer to the cabin. I'm doing something really stupid by coming here. I know I'm potentially leading the enemy to us, but I have to do this. A life saved is a life owed and Ethan saved my life many times in that place, even if he doesn't remember doing it.

This is going to hurt...

A lot.

<u>Ethan</u>

The anti-fae alarm or whatever it is starts going off and I almost fall out of the bed in my shock. Jackie is sleeping soundly next to me on the bed, and Max jumps out of the folding chair heading for the window.

"Uh... E-man, you up?" Shaun calls from the living room. I hear the cock of the shotgun before he says, "If you are, you might want to come out and talk to our guest. She's asking for you and swears it's just to talk."

Max growls but nods at me that it should be alright. I'm not so sure. I got the babies and Jack to worry about and a fae is in the freaking cabin... I can feel the panic start to rise, but Max grounds me, shoving Mr. Whiskers into my arms.

"Stabby is made of dirty steel. Mr. Whiskers will protect you from them," Max says as he pushes me toward the door. "I'll watch Jack, make sure they aren't pulling a switch or something."

I nod and slowly make my way down the little hallway. The cabin isn't big. It's only like five, maybe ten steps from the bedroom to the living room, but I shuffle step ten into a hundred. I don't want to see the faerie that wants to take me away from my family because of a freaking selfish Dick from over a decade ago.

"Been a long time, Ethan,"

My head shoots up and I'm not shuffling anymore. I fly through the air into the arms of the only fae person I ever met face to face, and the only one I could ever consider a friend. My laughter and joy turn to sorrow at the thought that she might have to take me away from here. I don't want her to be the one to hurt me and my babies...

I can't stop the sobs as I cling desperately to her. I don't want to let her go. I don't want hear to say she's here to take me away. We can just stay like this and nothing will change. It's a happy moment and I don't want that to change.

"Happy moments only last forever in our memories," she whispers into my ear before she straightens up from the hug. I forgot how much taller than me she is. She's not Max tall, but she's over six foot. "Right now, we need to face the issues at hand. But first, can you stop burning me with your teddy bear?"

I jump back and she turns to show me a burn on her back in the vaguest shape of Stabby. It was able to reach her through Mr. Whiskers. Before I can start to feel bad about it, she faces me with a smile. "It's a perfect disguise for a weapon against us. Keep it close until we figure this out."

Shaun seems to decide she's not a threat and props the shotgun next to his seat in the recliner. He's going to be playing guard for this interaction, I see. Well, I guess I should make introductions...

"Shaun, this is Celeste," I point to her and she bows in his direction causing me to giggle a bit. I stress giggle, big whoop. "Celeste, this is Shaun sitting in the chair and the teddy who burned you is Mr. Whiskers... Well, he didn't burn you... Stabby did, but Mr. Whiskers holds Stabby for me, so..."

She places her finger over my lips and I shut up. I guess I do ramble a lot. Is that an ADHD thing like my dad was talking about or is it just an Ethan thing like the mind and memory stuff? I'll have to ask and find out at some point, but I don't want to talk to them just yet. They didn't help me... I mean they didn't know I needed help, but they still weren't there.

"They knew," both Celeste and Shaun say simultaneously. They both look extremely angry as well, but the look they share is one of understanding and suddenly I have the feeling that my family would do well to not get on their bad sides.

Shaun stands up and heads to the kitchen. "Anyone want a drink? Ethan, Sprite or tea?"

It really shows how much one statement can change a person's mind because Shaun went from holding her at gunpoint to showing his back to her in under a minute.

"I'll take a peppermint tea if you have it," Celeste says and I drop to the seat of the couch. I can feel my breaths coming quicker and hold Mr. Whiskers tighter. It's not that night. I'm not there. The solid weight of Stabby inside of the bear helps to ground me in the present. After a few moments, I'm mostly alright, except a little sticky from the sweat that apparently broke out.

Celeste is looking at me in concern, but Shaun just places a teacup and a Sprite in front of us. He sits back in his chair with a bottle of beer in hand and says to our guest, "No P-mint in this house for reasons, as you can see. I hope chamomile is alright." He indicates toward the teacup with a nod of his chin before taking a swig from his bottle.

She gives me one last worried glance before picking up the cup and taking a sip. Once that happens, the atmosphere in the room has become a million times more relaxed. Max even comes out of the bedroom, leaving the door cracked so we will hear if Jack gets up. I don't understand what just happened here.

"Laws of hospitality are very important to the fae," Max tells me, not taking his eyes off of Celeste. There's suspicion in his gaze, but not hostility. At least not outright anyways. "Being offered food or drink and accepting creates a contract that one cannot harm the other in any way during the visit."

"You know our ways?" Celeste asks him with a searching gaze. She is looking for something in him. It's almost like she can see inside of him. She's like a built in x-ray or something.

Giggling that musical laugh I love to hear, she corrects me by saying, "I am looking to see if there is any of our blood in his ancestry. Most fae-born children raised by other kinds tend to be more wary of those of us who grow up in the courts. Blood calls to blood, which is how I knew you had some fae in you, Ethan."

What? I'm fae? What next... am I a zombie too? An Elephant? Hell at this point, I might as well just be a freaking god-spawn with how much is mixing around inside of me. Can't I just be normal?

I surprise everyone by breaking down into tears. I don't get why they're all surprised. I cry at everything now. Isn't that what pregnant people do? Eat, cry, throw up, and repeat. That's going to be my life for the next...

"How long will I be pregnant?" I ask looking at Shaun. I vaguely notice a gasp from Celeste next to me, but Shaun looks at me head to toe before asking, "When was your last heat?"

"Mid-January," says Max. "Started on the thirteenth. Ended on the seventeenth."

Everyone in the room looks at him with a mixture of surprise and confusion. I know I'm confused. Why in the fuck is Max tracking my heats?

He levels me with a glare and a smile before saying, "I'm head of security and the Alpha and his mate need to be in lockdown for the pack's safety for days on end. Yeah, I track your heats."

Ok that makes sense, I guess. But something tells me that isn't the real reason. I don't know what it is, but I know it makes me sad. Damn baby hormones making my eyes all wet again.

Shaun looks like he's doing some mental calculations in his head. I just sip my sprite and wait for him to answer my question. I need to know how long I'll be like this. I don't like not being in control of my emotions normally. Now, I have to compete with the babies and my fucked up brain to keep up the appearance that I'm not completely insane.

"None of us made it out unscathed, hun" Celeste mutters to me as she pulls me to her side. "You were in there longer than any of us. You're entitled to be as fucked up as you need to be."

Shaun glares at her, but I feel a sense of relief at her words. Since I got out, everyone has been doing their best to try and make me happy and not upset me. They all feel bad when I have my episodes, so I try not to have them. I don't want to make them feel sad or upset or angry, so I try not to let them see how I feel most of the time.

They mean well, but it's so hard to always hide it all away... the anger, the hurt, the betrayal... They're all happier when I am the sassy smart ass that they've always known, so that's who I am, but is Celeste right? Am I allowed to just let it out? Am I allowed to be broken?

"You're NOT broken," Max snarls, staring at his beer like it holds the secrets of the universe. "You can't be broken," he whispers. "I can't fix broken people. I can't lose you, too."

I don't even know if that last part was out loud, but I heard it loud and clear. Max needs me to not be broken. I'm not broken. For Max, I won't be broken.

"Alright, to answer your question," Shaun breaks into the silence, "Were pregnancies are the same length as human so it should technically be a total of ten months..."

"I thought it was nine months." I break in. I mean, I know I missed eight years, but basic historic biology didn't change that much.

He chuckles a bit before continuing, "It's closer to ten months, but most pregnancies aren't viable or detectable for the first month or so and miscarriages happen without the mother even realizing they are pregnant in the first place. They think they just had a really bad menstrual cycle and no baby...

"But back to you," he says, taking a swig from his bottle before resting his forearms on his legs, leaning forward and staring at the label of the bottle. "I can't really say with certainty how long you're going to carry. See, the omega thing means you're going to go into labor closer to the eight month mark just due to the fact that the birthing canal for omegas tends to be narrower and less flexible than in women. Add in the fact that it's twins, and we can almost guarantee premature labor."

I'm starting to get a little worried, so Celeste starts sending her little sparks into me to calm me down. This always worked in the lab. She has this weird feeling touchy healing thing she can do, but she never let the d-words in the lab see it. It means a lot that she trusts Shaun enough to use it in front of him.

"He's a doctor?" she asks in shock, pulling back from me. "And you trust him?"

I push myself back into her side and sigh, "He may be a d-word but he's also my bestest friend in the whole world. I told you about him. He's the secret partner, my fellow crusader. We just never got around to getting the capes and masks and all. But I mean he got the secret lair for us..."

She laughs and relaxes again, pulling me closer to kiss the top of my head. "Of course, I remember your bestie. Only people you talked about more were your big brother and his friends. The spicy chocolate one and the big lug who always saved you."

Max looks at me with a funny expression on his face. I don't think I've ever seen that look from him. I don't know what to make of it, but he hides it before I can ask.

"Yeah, sure, nice to know you've heard of me," Shaun says. There's no need to be rude.

"Point is, we got at least five months before you have to worry about anything, ok E-man?"

I nod my head, able to relax a bit with knowing I'm going to be normal for at least one thing in my life. I don't have to worry about anything like a two year pregnancy or anything weird like that.

"Back to the matter at hand," Max says as he gets up to grab another beer from the fridge. I lift up my empty can to indicate I need another Sprite. He shakes his head, but still grabs me another. I crack it open as he sits and continues on, "What the hell is up with your people going after Jack and Ethan?"

I thought we know why they're after me? Max gives me a look that very clearly says, "Shut up" but I didn't say anything... oh. That's right. My ability is all wonky right now and I can't control when I am broadcasting or not.

Celeste finally succumbs to the laughter she was trying so hard to hold in. I don't get what's so funny. It's not like I want to be like this. I never asked for anything special. I didn't want to be a freak. I only ever wanted to be normal and have a mommy and daddy who loved me. I want my Daddy, but he doesn't want me anymore.

I race out of the room to the bedroom, but stop in the doorway. I forgot Jackie was sleeping on the bed. I can't wake him up. I can't take up the bathroom in case someone needs it. I'll just go out in the yard. Shaun said his whole property is warded. I'll be fine.

I grab a blanket and climb out of the window, leaving it cracked a bit so I can come back in. I just need some time by myself. I want my Daddy back, but I screwed up so badly. I shouldn't have left.

Daddy? Can you talk to me, please?

I hope I can get through. I hope he doesn't ignore me.

I'm so lost in my own thoughts that I don't notice someone behind me. I barely register the little sparks of magic on my skin before darkness consumes my mind.

29

Unburied

Ric

Grabbing my phone, I immediately dial Max. Something is wrong. Something happened to my boy. Max is supposed to be there to stop it.

"What is it, Bossman?" Max says in greeting. He doesn't seem worried or tense at all.

"Where is Ethan?" I growl out. "Please tell me you have eyes on him and I am just being paranoid."

I can hear Max moving around, "He was a bit upset and ran to the bedroom a couple minutes ago. There's a lot going on, but he's gotta be the one to tell you the news."

The sound of a door opening is followed quickly by my warriors shocked and angry "Fuck!"

I can hear multiple sets of footsteps approaching and Jackie mumbling in the background.

I can tell the phone is being passed off to someone and the howl of Max's wolf comes through from a distance. My warrior is on the hunt for him. I have faith in Max, but if my boy is missing, I need to be a part of the search. My wolf is itching to break out, but I need to stay in control for just a little bit longer.

"Is this Ethan's mate?"

This is the voice of a fae. What the fuck is a fae doing in the same room as my baby brother? I don't hold back the growl this time.

"Relax, Alpha," the voice says. "I am called Celeste and I am in your mate's debt many times over so you and yours have no reason to fear me as long as you hold Ethan's favor."

I don't really relax, but my wolf does. Apparently, these words from this fae truly means Jackie is safe with her... at least I think they're a her? I don't have time to consider the gender of a fae.

"Do you know where Ethan is?" I snarl into the phone. I can hear the plastic and glass starting to crack in my grip, so I set it on the night stand and push the speakerphone. I know it will alert Bennet and Edward and right now I need the backup. They care just as much about my boy's safety as I do.

"I fear my brother may be trying to curry favor with the princeling even after everything I told him at the hospital. I swear to you on the ancestors we share that I did not know it was Ethan we were sent to collect, not until I laid eyes on him."

So they are here to collect from my father's fucked up deal. There has to be a way out of it that doesn't result in a war. We haven't found anything yet on our end, but maybe this Celeste can help us.

"What do you know of the deal that was made for Ethan? Do you know of any way out of it?" I ask her in desperation. Bennet and Edward are standing in the hall outside. I can feel the tension from them even through the closed door. "Is there a chance to end this without bloodshed?"

She seems to think for a moment before answering, "As long as there is no fae life lost, there is always a loophole. We cannot lie, but there must be fair exchange. A life for a life. How likely is it that Ethan will fight back?" She seems to be very clinical in her speech and thinking. Is this how all fae are? Why are they so compelling, then?

"Oh he'll fight back," says Shaun as I hear the cocking of a shotgun over the line. "His temper, once activated, is unrivaled."

"But will he kill, even by accident?" she asks him, seemingly ignoring me on the other end of the phone call.

"He can't kill," I tell them, the rage in my voice coming through loud and clear. "He won't kill, not even by accident... Does he have Stabby with him?" If he's armed, he'll be fine. We might have a mess to clean up, but he will be fine...physically.

There's a sound of footsteps retreating and returning before Shaun says, "Mr. Whiskers is here with us."

My heart sinks. Without his bear, Ethan is weaponless. Yeah, he'll heal anything they do to him, but without a blade, and without the ability to run away, he can't do anything to defend himself that couldn't accidentally kill someone. We never really got around to the hand-to-hand self defense sessions...

"Ric?" I hear my little brother's voice.

"Yeah Jackie bear?" I say. I know they have me on speaker for him to have heard me.

"I think someone took Tony," he says in his sleepy voice. The little man isn't fully awake or aware of anything right now.

"Where'd you put him, Jackie?" Shaun asks. I'm glad he's being gentle with my brother. He's a downright ass to me. "Did you leave him in the bag?"

"Nuh uh. I wrapped him in the blanket, but the blanket's gone too."

"How about you take Ethan's teddy and keep him safe for him

and we'll find your Tony for you?" Celeste asks as I hear some blankets being moved around.

Jack mumbles something that sounds in the affirmative and I can hear footsteps and a door clicking shut.

"My brother will pay for this," Celeste growls in a way that almost makes me want to make her pack. That growl would make any wolf proud. "Felix is a fucking idiot if he thinks Uncle Kestion gives two shits about us or keeping his word."

"You should probably get out here, Alpha." Shaun says to me, taking the phone off speaker. "Bring whoever you need to, but Celeste and Jack and I can't leave this house until everything is settled."

Before I can ask why, the call disconnects. Bennet and Edward come into the room and we know all three of us are going. It's just a matter of who else do we call in for this.

30

Unburied

Ric

Finding the turnoff for the cabin is actually more difficult in the daytime than I thought it would be. The foliage and terrain really do hide the start of the drive and the trees block the first turn so unless you know where to turn off the road, you'd never see it. I don't know if it's magic or creative landscaping or a mixture of both, but I'm thoroughly impressed and my wolf wants this man to join our pack.

We are greeted by a skinny young man holding a shotgun standing in the doorway. He eyes all of us before beginning introductions.

"I'm Shaun Cleary, formerly of the Jameson pack, white witch and half wolf, shaman to those who need it - and deserve it. No harm to me or mine and you are welcome to my home Alphas Heartstone and Jameson and King Edward. Break guesting laws and you will most definitely regret it."

There's a heaviness to the surrounding air for a few seconds before it lifts. Suddenly, the air smells more vibrant and I can sense the other people in the cabin. I hadn't realized until that moment that he was all I could sense. Oh, yes. I would love to have him on my side, but I'm absolutely certain that I don't want him as an enemy.

I notice Connor sniffing the air with a strange look on his face. His expression goes from puzzled to excited when he lands eyes on Shaun. Well, that should make things easier, right?

Looking at Shaun, I'm not so sure. The young werewitch storms into the cabin leaving us all a bit dumbstruck at what just happened. Connor looks crushed. It doesn't happen often, but there are times when fated mates reject each other. It's usually a cautionary tale, but I get the feeling the reasons here are not some parable. Shaun hates Connor for some reason, and we don't have time to figure it out.

"Connor, how about you stay with the cars and I'll fill you in when we go to leave?" I suggest to alleviate the awkwardness of having to navigate them both in the same room while getting the information we need to save Ethan.

Leaving my Beta outside with the other warriors, I enter the cabin behind Edward and Bennet. Yeah, this is exactly what I would picture for a twenty one or twenty two year old kid having his own place. The mismatched furniture, the tables being held together with duct tape, the blankets stapled to the walls for insulation... I kinda hate that I never got to experience this kind of freedom...

But then again... I got to experience being there for Jackie and all of his firsts and it was kind of awesome and amazing to get to see that.

"OK assholes," Shaun says to call us to attention. This kid has zero shits to give for us and frankly, I don't hold it against him. I'm not sure about the vampire or the other Alpha, but I respect him for it.

"Celeste here knows where they should be and what should be happening. She says Ethan *should* be alright and not harmed as long as he doesn't offend them too much."

He levels us all with a look and we understand. For Ethan, offending someone isn't a matter of him not saying the wrong thing. It's a matter of whether the person he says it to has a sense of humor or not.

"So we're on a tight schedule then?" says Edward, voicing everyone else's thoughts. I don't know how well this Celeste knows my boy, but his grandfather certainly understands that Ethan's mouth will most certainly get him in trouble before we can get there.

"There is another complication," Celeste says. "Beyond the fact that Ethan is a smartass who doesn't know how to shut his mouth when he's nervous..."

OK so it seems like she really does know my boy. I both do and don't want to know the story of how they know each other, but now isn't the time. We need to know what this other complication is. Shaun and Celeste seem to be having an argument without speaking. Edward looks like he's concentrating on something. Maybe he's trying to reach out to Ethan?

"You can quit trying to invade my mind, vampire," Shaun says suddenly. "I'm aware you're his gramps and all but he still has patient doctor confidentiality with me. He didn't want any of you to know, so I'm not going to say it."

"Well, I'm not his doctor!" Celeste yells at him, poking him in the chest. I can hear Connor's growl from outside... interesting.

"He doesn't want them to know! He wants to be the one to tell them, especially him!"

"We don't have that luxury now! Kestion will cut them out if he finds out!"

Edward falls back into a chair and the silence in the room is deafening. I didn't quite catch what this is about, but there's a secret and it involves Ethan and ... them?

I can see when it registers to Bennet. The look of joy on his face turns to horror as he turns to Edward. The vampire nods and looks to me. I can tell my face shows my confusion and fear. I need to know, but if this is the reaction from these two men, I get the feeling it will destroy me.

"NO!" Shaun yells, getting in the vampire's face, breaking our eye contact. "YOU don't get to share Ethan's secrets! Of all people in this room, you don't get to do a damn thing!"

The rage pouring off of him is drowning. I can feel my wolf struggling to keep us in our human shape. Shaun is out of control right now and if something doesn't calm him down quickly, we're going to have a lot of raging out wolves in a small area.

The door slams open and Connor throws himself at Shaun knocking him to the floor, holding him down as the kid struggles and screams against him. Looking at the others, I nod to the porch to indicate we should give them the room. I can hear my Beta saying something to him, but I can't decipher it over the screams.

Once we are all on the porch with the exception of Celeste, who went back to the bedroom to watch over Jack, we can all breathe a bit easier with the closed door between us and Shaun's anger.

"And that," says Edward, wiping his brow, "is why witches and werewolves should not mix."

I didn't even know vampires could sweat. I don't know if he actually perspired, but it's obvious that Shaun worried even him.

"What is that supposed to mean?" growls Connor as he comes

through the door looking a lot worse for the wear. It's not just his clothes or the scratches I can see healing on his face and arms. He looks like he just aged a decade and had his soul ripped out.

I reach for him and he smacks my hand away, shaking his head. I get it. He doesn't want any comfort.

Edward acts like he's seen nothing out of the ordinary and just answers the question.

"Witches get their power from emotions mostly. Werewolves need to be in control emotionally to keep the balance between their sides. When you combine the two, you get what you see..."

He pointedly looks away from Connor to continue, "a young, uncontrolled child who could kill us all by accident if he gets too emotional. If raised under a kind and honorable Alpha, some-times they survive and become stable. Outside of that? They are usually too dangerous to be allowed to live."

The growl from Connor isn't unexpected, but I am surprised at the one from Bennet and my own wolf.

"That boy in there risked his own life for my son these days! He is under my protection," Bennet growls out to the apparent surprise of the vampire.

"Not that I should have to say it," I interject, making sure the vampire is looking at me and not my Beta, "But he's obviously the fated mate to my Beta, Ethan's brother, as well as being Ethan's best friend. Do you really think it's smart to threaten him when you just got your grandson back in your life?"

Edward looks like I just struck him. This is why everyone hates the vampires. It's not their strength or speed or even the feeding on blood that bothers us all. It's the way they stop thinking about people after a while. He loves Ethan because he's his grandson, but everyone else doesn't matter to him unless he's forced to see them as important.

"If Ethan didn't view me as a brother, would you even let *me* live?" Connor asks him. "I'm the spawn of the evil things that destroyed him long before that lab got ahold of him. They loved me but did that to him! Don't I deserve to die, too?"

I watch my best friend fall to his knees right in front of us. Whatever happened inside broke him irreparably. Even when we thought Ethan was dead, I didn't see this level of pain in him. We stand silently by and wait for his tears to stop. Both the men standing next to me are looking at Connor in pity. It's almost like they know his pain, but neither of them had fated mates, unless...

I look at Edward in dawning horror and he nods at me.

His mate has rejected him. The only pain worse in this world is to find out they no longer live and that you are at fault.

Bennet looks over to me and nods as well.

We both know the pain all too well and would not wish it on another, even an enemy.

I look back to my Beta who is shakily trying to get to his feet. When I try to help him stand, he pushes me away forcefully. "Call me when you're ready to get my brother back, or don't. I can't wait here."

He doesn't even bother to undress before he shifts and runs off into the trees. Moments later, I hear his wolf's howl. I've only heard a sound like that once before and that was my grandmother the day she found my grandfather's body. He died in the attack. She died of a broken heart upon finding him. I never understood how my father stayed strong until this year. I have been trying to live up to a lie all this time. He was never strong. He didn't show any grief because he didn't feel it.

Looking at the two men before me, I wish I had known them both sooner. I wish everything hadn't been so fucked up and Ethan got a normal life and then we'd be family and not this broken thing in the middle of the woods.

The door opens and a very haggard and red-eyed Shaun motions us back in the room. He looks around and seems almost disappointed not to find someone else out here with us. He made his own bed with this and I hope he can handle the consequences of it. The prospects of him joining my pack have dropped significantly, but I won't deny him if he requests it. What he has done for Ethan and Jack have already earned my trust. Connor will have to find a way if Ethan wants Shaun close.

"Ok so let's just agree that no sharing of Ethan's secret will be happening via words or thoughts and I should be able to hold back the anger. Deal?" he says as he takes his seat in the recliner. He looks like he hasn't slept in a week, even though less than thirty minutes ago, he was in perfect health.

I've already nodded my agreement, but Bennet and Edward exchange a look. It's a tense minute or so before they both nod. Shaun relaxes in his seat and calls Celeste to rejoin us.

"You need to go NOW," she says as she comes out of the bedroom with a huge sword. Where did that come from? I look to Shaun in alarm and he's just as surprised as I am. "The word has gone out that my brother has Ethan and because of the reward in place for his capture, my brother doesn't stand a chance. He is sworn to protect Ethan and see he comes to no harm in transport. It was the best I could get out of him without tipping my hand. The others are not and will not be gentle. He can't afford to be injured."

She shares a look with Shaun. It's obvious she wants to tell us more, but she trusts him on this. I hope it doesn't backfire on my boy.

"Alpha Alaric Jameson, mate of Ethan Sinclair, you have the power to track them," she says to me and a heaviness falls over the room. "You shall find him only if your heart is true."

"Alpha Bennet Heartstone, father of Ethan Sinclair, you have the power to save them," she says to Bennet, and the air thickens even more. "You will know when the blood shall be spilled."

She turns to Edward last. He raises an eyebrow but does not interrupt or stop her in any way.

"King Edward Sullivan, father of Elizabeth Welling, grandfather of Ethan Sinclair, you have the power to reach them in time... You must share power or all will be lost this night."

The pressure is so much now that I can't even take a breath. Celeste drags her finger down the blade of her sword leaving a streak of red on the edge of the blade. Once her finger leaves the metal, the tension breaks and I'm wondering what the fuck just happened.

"Fae prophecy. Very rare," says Edward. "True named and all. OK so I'm guessing I'm sharing vamp speed which means, it's just us three going on this trip. I can't share with more."

Celeste collapses to the couch in exhaustion. The sword is nowhere in sight. "You got it, Gramps. Now get your asses going or you'll be too late."

Edward pulls out a dagger and pricks the tip of his finger. He drops a single drop of blood into two glasses on the table and then fills them a bit with water. The blood dissolves almost instantly leaving the water with a slight pink tinge.

"Drink up," he says. "This will only work for you to because you are bound to one of my blood by blood."

I'm a bit confused by that, but we don't have time to worry about it. I need to find my boy right now. I down the water like it's a shot and I can feel the buzz throughout my body. Bennet does the same and we both look at Edward like he's got the next clue.

Shaun speaks up from his chair. He at least has some of his color back now. "Your turn, Loverboy. Go find my best friend."

That's right. I can track him only if my heart is true. There's only one thing I know in my heart without a shadow of a doubt right now and that is that I love Ethan, my boy, my Blue, my little bluebird. I pick up Mr. Whiskers and suddenly I can feel my boy. It's almost like there's a string in my chest pulling me to him.

I don't even wait for the others. I take off out the door, clutching the damn teddy bear to my chest. My boy needs me. He needs us all.

31

____

Unburied

<u>Ethan</u>

OK so I much prefer the wakeup from drugs compared to the wakeup from a magic knockout. All the pain, but none of the floaty feelings. Zero stars... do not recommend. Then again, drugs and pregnancy are a big no no from what I understand, so it's probably better that they didn't use drugs.

"You're pregnant?!"

I jump a bit at the voice and turn around to see a guy that kinda looks like Celeste. I mean he looks familiar, is that why? No... he's the guy from the hospital parking lot.

"You're Felix?" I ask him instead of answering. My wolf is telling me that I shouldn't let any fae know I'm pregnant if I want to get out of this in one piece with my babies. "I'm pretty sure I'm friends with your sister."

"We cannot be friends with those who are inferior," he spits out, but I can tell he doesn't believe what he's saying. It doesn't smell like a lie exactly, but more that he doesn't really believe that anyone is actually inferior.

"Yeah, you don't believe that," I say to him as I sit up and look around. I think we're in a hotel room. I don't really know since the only one I've ever been in was that really grungy motel where Ric cleaned me up after the basement with Pete. "So, where are we exactly? I don't really get out much and I would love to check more places off my bucket list."

Felix is looking at me like I've grown another head. *I'm actually growing two...maybe four... he he he.*

Dirty jokes aside, and honestly I shouldn't be making dirty jokes about my babies, but he really is looking at me strangely. Do I not act like a typical kidnap victim? Should I be scared?

"Do you even know the shit I've been through in my life?" I ask him. "You are the least scary thing I've woken up to in the last twenty years and I'm only twenty one."

A knock on the door has him jumping and falling off the bed to the floor. I guess his sister got all the smarts and courage in the family. I stand to open the door for him. I mean, I'd rather face this shit head on rather than cower in a corner. I know Daddy is on his way. I can feel him getting closer. I told him I want him and he's coming. That's good enough for me.

So now I'm just playing my cards that I have until he can get here and make it all better.

Before I can even take a step toward the door, it's kicked open by a big brute of a man. I can smell the dirt on him. It's so strong I can almost taste it. I hate the taste of dirt. I don't like the memories this guy's scent is bringing up in me, so I sit back down and play the meek card. The ones who don't know me always think I'm weak. I always make the new ones force my submission. My wolf prefers it that way. It makes it easier for him to hold back and conserve our strength.

Do what you can to protect them, not me. I tell my wolf. I can feel his hesitation, but he agrees.

"Felix, buddy," comes a voice from behind the ogre. I think he's an ogre... maybe a she. I don't judge, but it looks like a he to me. I'm sure he'll correct me if he even speaks. I don't know anything about ogres.

"Did you really think you could get away with collecting the bounty on your own?" the voice asks. I recognize this voice. This is the smarmy one from Max's memory... the one who actually made the deal for me.

As they step around the ogre into the room, I kinda understand why Max had such a difficult time identifying them. The voice is bad enough, but their entire being screams androgenous as all fuck. It's going to bother the hell out of me if I don't ask and I kinda need to be paying attention here.

"Are you a male or female fae or does gender fluid apply? It's really going to bother the fuck out of me and I don't want to call you the wrong thing and offend you or nothing..." I'm trying to play up the country bumpkin schtick here since Felix pulled that high and mighty routine with me earlier. I figure most of the fae are going to be all full of themselves and such that it might buy me some points.

The strange fae smiles and I don't want to see him doing that anymore. I can't objectively say it's a bad smile. It's actually kind of a perfect smile... and that's what is wrong with it. It's too perfect. The teeth are too white, too straight, too even. The face is too smooth. There are no wrinkles or laugh lines or blemishes or anything. There's not a hair out of place.

This appearance is false, my wolf supplies.

Thanks, Captain Obvious, I reply in my head. I remember something Max once told me when I was little...

Everyone's got some ugly on them. If it's not showing on the outside, it has to be on the inside and inside ugly is dangerous ugly.

Yeah this fae is extremely dangerous then, because there is zero ugly on the outside. The chuckle that comes out of his throat sounds like music, but I want to cover my ears and scream. It's too pretty. Nothing in life is good for me. Nothing. I can't trust this fae at all.

"Very good, omega," they say to me with a more natural smile. "You have learned much from the world that most lesser beings take most of their lives to realize. And yet you managed in barely two decades."

He's just like the docs in the lab. I'm just a pet that learned a cute trick to him. Well, I played them and won. I just have to hold out a bit longer for Daddy.

"Alucard, I swear. I just wanted my sister and I to be free," Felix says falling to his knees in front of the other one. I guess their name is Alucard... weird name. "The money is yours. I just want our debts cleared from our father so that she can have a child freely."

"Oh poor Felix," Al tsks to the boy at his feet. "Your sister will be mine and her future children are my property to do with as I wish. That is what is promised to me when I hand over the mutt."

He kicks Felix in the face and I watch as the boy hits his head on the side of the dresser, blood spilling onto the carpet. I feel bad for the cleaning crew here. Blood is hell to get out...

Well in for a penny and all that. This Al dude says he's gonna control Celeste's baby bits? Take her kids from her? Force her?

FUCK THAT!

They did that enough to us at the lab. NO MORE. Time for me to find out if it's the G Lady or my father's blood that protects me. Fae can't get in trouble for harming another fae, right? I mean Al doesn't seem to be worried about it, so neither will I.

I pull the letter opener from the small of my back. I'm glad I remembered to grab it before going outside. I just wish I had one of my blades. Stabby would be great right about now. As I shift a bit on the bed, waiting for a chance, I feel something under my butt. Lifting up, I feel under me and pull out Tony. How in the fuck is he here?

Never mind that... did Ric take Junior out or leave him in for Jack? I feel for the hole in Tony's neck and can feel the hard butt of Junior on the tip of my finger. I have steel and silver... one for each hand. That should be enough.

Protect them, I send to my wolf as I launch myself at Alucard, bringing both blades down on his back. I hope I am able to sever the nerves and tendons quickly enough to not lose this fight. I don't have to win, necessarily, but I can't afford to lose.

Ric

Along the way, I can see I'm catching up to Max. I'm going too fast for him to keep up, but I feel like we'll need him so I grab him by the scruff and carry him along. He tries to fight me at first, but his wolf quickly realizes that it's his Alpha carrying him and he relaxes into the ride.

I feel the pull to my boy so strongly, but I stop in front of a mid class motel. We're somewhere in northern Georgia. I don't like that they were able to get Ethan so close to Atlanta already, but at least he's still here and not fully in their clutches yet. Max's wolf whines and mine is telling me that something smells off.

It's true. It smells of swamp and brine. There aren't any saltwater swamps this far inland or north. The smell is horribly out of place.

Edward and Bennet come to a stop next to me and look surprised to see Max's wolf.

"He was on the way," I shrug as I say it. They don't need to understand my instincts.

32

____

Unburied

<u>Ethan</u>

OK so maybe stabbing the fae thingy that I'm not sure what they actually are was a bad idea. The smell of swamp overpowers everything in the room as this horrid green goo starts pouring out instead of blood.

Note to future self... fae anatomy is totally different and blood isn't always blood.

The thing that calls itself Alucard throws me off him to the bed. It doesn't look anything like it did before. Yeah, He's an it now. There's not much resembling a dude anymore and it's not like I ever got an answer to my question before.

It dropped the extra pretty from before and now I can see the pointy teeth and the green tongue and the shiny eyebrows. I actually think it looks better like this, but right now ain't the time to be judging a beauty contest.

"Nice try, mongrel," Al says to me as it manages to pounce on top of me, pinning me to the bed. "But for that bit of flesh, I think I will give yours a try before I hand you over to our prince."

It looks at me like they're waiting for something. Felix is trying to get up and the ogre hasn't moved since he kicked the door down, but Al is just waiting. Are they waiting for me to be scared? Does it think that threatening to assault me is going to scare me?

"Oh. My. Gods!" I yell out. This is almost insulting. "Doesn't anyone do their fucking homework before kidnapping someone anymore?"

Al sits back on its heels and I can see the package ain't exactly normal, so I'm going to stall as long as I can. Daddy's close. I can feel it.

"Do you know where I ended up when my Uncle Carl double crossed Alpha Richard?" I ask to try and get more time.

It looks confused, so I go on. The longer I can keep everyone distracted with talking, the less I have to worry about doing damage repair later.

"Uncle Carl stole me away the same night you guys were supposed to get me from what I hear. He sold me to some lab for twenty K but then the dude in charge upped it to fifty when he found out I am an omega. Uncle Carl made bank and Alpha Dick got screwed over."

They're all listening, but I'm really only worried about making sure I don't have to have that weird looking thing inside me. Please hurry, Daddy...

"I spent eight years in that place where they cut me open, cut off pieces, made me fight others for their amusement. They also stole my virginity and repeatedly violated me in every possible way. Celeste knows what I'm talking about. You should ask her about that place."

I can see the moment it registers on its face that it knows of where I am talking about. Celeste got out somehow and I can only imagine the rest of the fae around her know at least some of the story.

"That place was destroyed. There are no records left. Who was in charge?" Al demands of me, leaning back over me. Some sort of goop drips off what used to be hair to land on the pillow beside me. The smell of rotting fish and saltwater is just too much for my newly queasy stomach and I end up projectile vomiting in its face, like that old movie where the girl's head spins around. Except this time isn't pea soup. It's the real deal.

After a moment of shock, Al slaps me across the face hard enough to see stars. I lick my lips and taste a little blood. Oh... I guess the time to talk is over.

Before I can retaliate in any way, a gigantic silver wolf growls from the doorway. In a single leap it pulls Al off of me and rips into his neck. I'm pretty sure this is my dad, but he's huge... like WAY bigger than Ric's wolf. He turns his back on Al and nuzzles into me to check me over. He licks my temple and I can almost feel something buzzing inside my head. The pain and dizziness starts to fade.

Did the douche nozzle give me a brain bleed? Was I actually in danger of dying from that slap?

I can't stop the growl that reverberates through the room. I hear my dad whine kinda through the haze that is my rage. This mother fucker almost killed my babies because of a little vomit?! If the bitch doesn't want people to puke around it, they need to control its fucking rotting fish goop hair better!

I pick Al up by its hair, or whatever it is and drag them to the door. It's still alive. They shouldn't die from this, but I can't stand to have the smell in the room any longer. I toss the body out the door and over the railing. I hear the thud of flesh hitting asphalt and turn back toward my father who is now naked and pulling on one of the robes from the bathroom.

Hearing a growl from below, I turn to the door in excitement, but then realize that wasn't Daddy's growl. It wasn't him. I let my shoulders fall and I shuffle towards the bed not covered in goop and vomit and go to sit down.

"He is here, you know," Bennet says to me. "Alaric is outside. You just have to go to him."

I want to jump up and run outside, but I remember... Daddy was mad at me...

"He wasn't mad at you, sweetheart," my father says. "He was angry at the situation, at himself, at the fates for putting this all on you. He was never mad at you."

"REALLY?!" I shout loud enough they probably heard me back in Ohio. Hell, for all I know we could be in Ohio again. I hope not. I don't have good memories there.

I run out of the door and almost launch myself over the railing. Looking down, I see Grandpa Eddie and a wolf that I think is Max standing over Al. It's still down for the count, so I'm not worried. I like seeing the smile on Gramps' face and the wolfy grin I'm getting from Max, but I don't see Daddy. Did he leave?

No way. Bennet wouldn't have told me at all if Ric wasn't going to stick around. I look to my left and there's no one. I look to my right, preparing myself to be disappointed...

DADDY! He's really here!

I run and jump into his arms and I'm never letting go ever again. He carries me back into the smelly room, but I don't care. I'm where I belong, in Daddy's arms. Where those arms happen to be doesn't matter.

Ric

Edward and Bennet sniff the air. Bennet wrinkles his nose at the smell, but Edward is starting to look scared.

"Blood has been spilled," he says turning to Bennet and the latter races up the stairs and to the door that is open to the night air. A horrible screeching wail echoes through the night and the brine smell intensifies. I can hear a wolf growling and another whining. The screeching is cut off when a body comes flying out of the door and lands in a heap in front of us.

Max snarls at the body in front of us. My wolf growls at him to stand down. This fae is still alive and must stay that way in order to keep Ethan safe... at least that's according to what Celeste had told us. I leave Max to guard the body and look to Edward. He is staring at the body on the ground with hatred in his eyes. He recognizes this one as well. It makes me wonder what role this one has played in my mate's ordeals.

I start to walk up the steps to the open room. I'm pretty sure the fae either killed everyone here or made sure the rest of the place was empty tonight. There's no way that this much noise wouldn't bring out at least one nosey human. There is talking coming from the room, but I'm still too far away to really make it out.

"REALLY?"

Ok my boy is fine. I let out the breath I didn't realize I was holding. I barely clear the top of the stairs when I see him run from the room. He looks down to the parking lot and frowns, then giggles, and frowns again. He keeps leaning over the railing further and further and I'm about to call out to him to be careful when he leans back on his feet again and looks to his left and right.

The look on his face when he sees me is one that I will cherish forever. I wish my mind was a camera and I could forever capture the beauty of his expression right then. Of course, he doesn't even give me time to cherish it before my arms are full of my little bluebird and I have to grab the railing to stop us from tumbling down the concrete stairs.

My happiness starts to fall as I feel the wetness on my neck and feel Ethan shaking in my arms. I'm worried that I've hurt him again and go to put him down, but he clings tighter. He's like a killer koala. He's not going to let go, but I need to find a way to make him not upset.

"Happy tears, Daddy," he whispers between hiccups. "These are happy tears. I knew you'd come."

33

Unburied

Ric

Entering the room, I'm expecting a warzone. But the only mess I can see is a bit of vomit and slime on one bed and a few puddles of swamp water on the floor. A couple small bloodstains are around the dresser, but from the smell, I know they weren't caused by Ethan's blood. Bennet is sitting in a chair, looking perfectly comfortable in a too short robe, while the two fae in the room seem to be figuring out something between them.

Right now, I'm more concerned with making sure my boy is alright than I am with whatever else is going on with the fae, so I sit down on the clean bed with him still clinging to me. Thinking I might want to breathe again some day, I pull the secret weapon from my back pocket and tap him on the shoulder with it.

He looks up at me in confusion and turns his head just enough to see...

"MR. WHISKERS!"

He snatches the bear from my hand so fast he almost falls off my lap to the floor. I catch him and manage to get him to turn around and sit next to me on the bed. He keeps his legs draped across mine and tucks himself into my side with one arm curled around the teddy and his other thumb is in his mouth. Of course it is. I kind of wish I had taken the time to get his hands wiped first, but what's done is done now.

The chuckle from the ogre surprises me. Their kind isn't generally known for laughter or conversation of any kind, really. I narrow my gaze at them, challenging them to make a comment against my boy.

"No offense, Alpha," says the other fae in the room. He bears a resemblance to Celeste, so I'm guessing this is her idiot brother. "It's just rare to see someone so openly embracing their child side in our presence. Edith here was just remarking that if he'd shown this side earlier, Alucard would have run away in fear. That one is actually afraid of children."

Edith chuckles again and nods towards the other bed and grunts something. I look to the other for a translation. Instead of saying anything, he goes to the vomit covered bed and roots around in the bedding pulling out a small switchblade and a letter opener and... Tony? How did Jack's tiger end up here?

I look down at my boy who is now making grabby hands towards the fae. When he tries to close the switchblade, he hisses and drops the knife on the ground. Ethan giggles as if it was a silly joke. "Silly, Fewix. Junior is all steely and burny for yous." He says with another giggle.

Bennet comes over and collects the other two items, carefully placing the letter opener on the table and then picks up the blade from the floor to close it. Once it's closed, he appears to be confused on where it's supposed to go. Ethan starts making the grabby hands at his father and is almost leaning out of my lap before Bennet hands them over.

We all watch as he feels around the neck of the tiger and then just slips the blade in. When his hand moves away, you couldn't even tell there was a hole there, let alone hiding a knife like that. Almost everyone is shocked, but Edith looks to be in awe. Yeah, my bluebird is really special.

"We go bad men, now?" Ethan asks when no one has said anything for a while. I try to make sense of why he's asking us to go to the bad men. We came here to stop him from going to them. Why in the hell would we of all people take him there?

Felix gives him a weird look and then asks, "What do you know that we don't?"

"Everything," my boy says pulling the thumb from his mouth. "I know everything and Al is not going to be in a good place when I'm fully done."

34

Unburied

Ric

We argued for a while up in that room that reeked of saltwater and vomit. There was enough time that Max managed to find some clothes and this Al fellow had mostly healed his wounds. Edward found some iron chains somewhere, so he's at least contained. We have him gagged and chained on the vomit bed because none of us wanted to sit there.

It's been long enough that Ethan has fully come back to his adult self, or at least as fully as he gets. He keeps insisting we need to go see this Prince Kestion ourselves and we have to do it now, before something is visible. I'm not following, but I trust my boy. I don't want him in danger, but he keeps insisting that this is the path that will bring all of us safely out the other side with no threats hanging over us.

Bennet and Edward are both against this, but this Felix fellow and Edith seem to agree with Ethan. We aren't counting their votes because well... they are both duty bound to bring Ethan in.

Max is the deciding factor here. He has been silent through the whole argument and now everyone is looking at him expectantly.

Edward expects him to go to their side, say we aren't going... that we're going to go back home and prepare for the next wave which may never come. I hope he sides with Ethan. Max has always supported and protected Ethan. He needs to have his back in this as well, but I can't force him. This has to be his decision. I trust him completely with my mate's safety and wellbeing.

"Are you sure about this little dude?" he asks looking Ethan in the eye.

"Sure as the fact that your dick swings to the right when you run," my boy says and I physically turn him in my lap to look at me.

"What was that?" I growl. "Why are you looking at another man's dick?"

I love the sound of Ethan's laughter, but this isn't the right time.

"Relax, Bossman," Max says, trying to hold back his own laughter. "It's something I said to him when he was a kid and then he asked a ton of questions about how big does it have to be to swing to one side and does that mean I have a limp or that my dick is stronger on one side rather than the other and can you exercise a dick to make it swing both ways and stuff like that..." He dissolves in laughter and has to crouch down, clutching his sides to wait for the chuckle fit to pass.

The rest of the room has also broken out in various forms of laughter and even I chuff a bit. Everyone needed the break in the tension. The only one not laughing is the asshat in the chains and I don't really give a flying fuck about him.

"If you're sure, then yeah. I'm with you." Max says as he's finally able to stand back up. "Anything you need from me, you know you always got it." He says wiping the moisture from under his eyes.

"Now that you mention it…"

What does my boy have planned?

Ethan

Getting everyone on board with just going was the hard part. Now that we're all committed, here comes the easy part. Shock and awe, baby. Isn't that the way to win these kinds of things?

We are just going to make sure that they have no reason to come after me anymore, first and foremost… But then we're also going to remind them of just who I'm related to and what can happen if they really try to push things. Right now, I just can't decide which one I want to present first…

I think about it for the whole drive into the city of Atlanta. I saw a bit of the area when I was here in the summer, but I didn't pay much attention to anything but getting to the airport back then. But this time, I don't have the luxury of sight seeing either. I need to make up my mind which way I want to play this. Either way, the outcome will be the same. Right now, it's just a matter of mitigation of damages.

Becoming a papa looks good on you.

Grandpa Eddie's voice in my head makes me jump. I look through the rearview to see him and my father in the second car with Edith. Gramps is smiling at me. If Shaun went and blabbed his mouth, I'm going to kill him. This is my news to share, not his!

Your friend kept his word and almost killed us all when I figured it out. He is a loyal and true friend to you and I'm glad you had his protection.

I face back forward in my seat, smiling a bit to myself. I'm really happy my grandpa likes my best friend. I'm not too sure how my best friend feels about my grandfather, but half is better than none.

We pull into an underground garage and park. Felix turns around in the seat and warns me, "Please don't talk to the prince the way you spoke to Alucard. He will do much worse than slap you for the disrespect."

Ric growls at the threat and says "He can try, but to hit Ethan is to call for war with my pack."

"And mine," says Bennet as he opens my door for me to let me out of the car.

"I don't think we need to even say it," says Grandpa Eddie as he comes walking up to us, Edith's arm in his. Maybe he doesn't need to meet the kindly secretary lady at the school after all...

Felix shakes his head and mumbles, "Don't say I didn't warn you," and leads the way to a wooden door in the shadow of the stairwell.

"Where are we exactly?" Max asks as he takes position on my right. Ric is on my left. Gramps is in front and Dad is behind. Why are they surrounding me like this?

"The entrance to our kingdom, or at least the side entrance." Felix explains as he places his hand on the wood. It glows slightly before it creaks open a tiny bit. He uses his fingernails to get enough purchase to pry it the rest of the way open. "Edith and I aren't highborn enough to use the front door. Celeste can pass because she's got suitors who insist she appears higher than our blood actually is."

The hall beyond the door is dark and musty. It smells like it's underground and I don't see any kind of support system and I don't want to be buried again. I don't like that at all. I don't want to go in there...

I don't realize I'm backing up until I feel my father's hands resting on my shoulders.

"Is there another way we can go that isn't underground like this?" Ric asks looking at me, not Felix.

"He's not going into an unsupported tunnel," Max says before the fae can answer.

Edith pulls out a phone and turns on the flashlight. She shines it into the doorway and we can see that about three feet higher than the doorway is a stone arch that runs the length of the ceiling as far as can be seen. We just couldn't see it without the light shining on it.

"Are you ok to go in?" Ric asks me seriously. I know if I say I can't do it, he'll find another way. Max is looking at me like he will go in and drag this prince out to me if I asked him to. I know it's going to look silly, but there's only one way to be sure I can make it through this tunnel without breaking apart again.

I pinch my nostrils together and answer in a nasally voice, "I can manage."

Gramps giggles at that and picks up the waste of space that is Al from where he dropped them when I stopped.

35

Unburied

Ethan

Felix leads the way with some sort of light shining ahead on the floor so we don't trip. Edith brings up the rear, using her phone as a spotlight above us until it flickers and goes out. Did she forget to charge it or something? It's a bit scarier without the extra light.

Felix turns to the right at what appears to be a solid marble wall and again, pushes his hand on it. I have to admit it's kind of cool that they have security like this. I wonder if it would work for me and dad with our little bit of fae blood.

The smile Felix gives me over his shoulder says that yes it would. Also, it tells me that I'm broadcasting. Shit. I need to shut that shit down if I want to pull this off.

The room we enter is huge. We are obviously underground and yet somehow there is sunlight coming in the room... sunlight? It's supposed to be night time.

Time moves differently in faerie. Just keep your thanks to yourself and don't eat or drink until one of us gets an oath that it is safe to do so, but don't refuse to take refreshments if offered. Gramps is trying to give me a quickie lesson on dealing with the fae. What he doesn't know is that Celeste and I went over all of this way back in the day when we were in the basement of the lab, waiting for our turns to fight.

At the end of the room appear to be a couple more ogres. I wonder if Edith knows them. Looking back at her, I can see her turning her nose up at them. Huh… seems like she doesn't care for them too much. When I look to the front again, the ogre on the left seems to have slumped a bit. That's interesting…

"Well met, visitors," comes a voice from behind the ogres. What is it with these fae thinking that it's cool to talk from behind someone else. It's not cool. It's just rude. We should be able to see who is speaking, it's only polite.

"Since when does a prince need to be polite to his belongings, omega?" he asks stepping out from behind his guards. I can't say I'm all that impressed. Just like Al, he's too pretty and that tells me that he's either ashamed of his true appearance or he's hiding something that he can't afford to have seen. At least Al had the excuse of making sure no humans saw him. We're all supes in here, so what does it matter?

A whining growl comes from the front of the room and the ogres and Felix fall to the floor in supplication. Max, Ric, and Bennet all seem to be fighting to keep their wolves at bay and Gramps is not looking on the fae prince dude kindly. In fact, he looks like he wants to rip his head from his shoulders, but that would only incite a war.

"Look Prince Dude, we're not here to fight." I say to try to break the tension. It breaks alright, but only because the shock of being addressed so informally seems to momentarily stun him. I continue before he can finish his reboot.

"You might want to stop and think about who you'd be fighting if you keep coming after me. My mate is the Alpha of the Jameson pack. My father is the Alpha of the Heartstone pack. And my Grandfather here, is the King of the Eastern US Vampires. You know, the very king you pay tribute to so that he doesn't allow other supes to invade and attack those of your people and businesses that live outside of the mounds you've built..."

My speech makes him pause. It also makes everyone else in the room stare at me like I've become someone else. I'm not dumb. Just because I barely finished the eighth grade doesn't mean I am stupid. My best friend is a freaking genius and I kept up with him just fine until I was sold.

At that thought, the prince dude looks at me. Shit, I'm broadcasting again.

"Who sold what was mine by right?" he demands it of us, but no one answers him.

"WHO WAS IT?"

He's furious not only that I was sold, but that none of us will answer him. I feel bad for Edith and Felix. This seems to be hurting them. I don't want to hurt anyone. That's why I made us come here.

"No one sold what was yours," I say to him and he looks confused.

"But you are mine, omega." Yeah I can't help the growls around me this time. I have a hard enough time holding back my own wolf.

"Actually, I'm not," I say to him. "You weren't there for the deal that was struck. Did you get the exact words from the memory of one who was there?"

He goes from angry to confused to thoughtful before he answers.

"The agreement was with Richard Jameson, son of Alpha Alistair Jameson, when he ate of my food without my blessing as he visited an establishment of the night here in my city. He pledged a firstborn son of Alpha blood. When Alucard and Reese were sent to collect, they told me Richard promised an omega in the place of his son and himself. That omega is you. The deal was struck and accepted. You are mine."

I tap my finger against my chin to draw it out a bit. Yes, I'm being a bit of a smartass, but I can't help it. This prince dude really doesn't know how to deal with his own people if he managed to let this one slip by him.

"Your people didn't tell you the whole truth, nor did they ask the right questions when the deal was struck. It's why they were chasing him down when I was stolen out from under them… Gramps, can you share Max's memory with the class, pretty please?"

At his smile, I see that Gramps has finally caught on to why we are here and why I insisted on this meeting. We can end this stupid me being bought or sold or traded off thing once and for all.

36

Unburied

Ethan

I watch the prince dude's reactions to the memory. At first he seems very bored, but when it gets to the point where Dick assures Al and the other guy that I don't have family that will care if I'm given to them, it's obvious that we've won. As the memory ends, the prince dude sits roughly on his throne.

His glamour falls away and he looks a bit older, but much nicer now. Yeah the eyes are a bit freaky with the rainbow thing going on and the purple tint to his skin isn't typical, but I'd say he's quite handsome this way.

Ric's growl from beside me makes me giggle. What can I say? I'm not dead. I can look.

The prince seems to get an idea that he feels might help him get what he wants. He is sitting up straighter, with a look of triumph on his face. I hope we can counter it since what he wants is me. "At the time the deal was struck, you had no family to claim you, though. The Alpha spoke the truth at that time."

He looks positively proud of himself. By fae law that is enough. Celeste told me that the fae are bound by the words spoken at the time they are spoken. So yeah, no one wanted me back then. Shit...

"Richard knew I am Ethan's grandfather!" Grandpa Eddie says forcefully, stepping forward to block me from the view of the prince dude. "He knew I was coming for my grandson after he gained his wolf. He was well aware of these things as they were arranged at Ethan's birth and he was in the room when I personally set everything up with Alistair."

The prince still doesn't look like he cares, but Edward leans forward with a smug look when he says, "Richard lied to your emissaries and therefore everything promised is null and void as it was based on a known lie."

Gramps for the save! He looks to me and gives me a wink. It feels really good to have family at my back now. I mean, I think they all have my back. I hope so anyways. At least I know I got Gramps in my corner.

"I will NOT give up my claim!" the prince yells out, rising from his throne, sending everything from the side table flying. "Guards! Evict them all from the mound but the omega!"

As the two ogres approach us, Edith pushes to her feet and stands in the way. They seem hesitant to go through her, but the prince orders, "Kill any who attempt to stop you from following my orders!"

This is my only shot. I just hope it works enough to get her attention. I jump in front of Edith before any blow can land. Squeezing my eyes shut tight, I brace for the pain of a blow... only it doesn't come.

I open my eyes to see the room frozen in time. I can tell that Grandpa Eddie is aware of what is going on, but he can't seem to interact at all. That's fine. I just needed to get her here to intervene a little bit and she's here. Time for some recompense for playing me for a fool. But first... acting time.

"Hey there G Lady! Been a while."

My child, a Goddess's time is very precious. Why have you called me here?

"So, here's the deal. This fae prince dude wants to claim me and take me and make me a sex slave or something and kill all my family, but I want him to call off his bogus claim since we disproved that he ever had a valid claim to begin with. Now, he's throwing a fit and if he keeps on, I'm gonna have to kill him and that goes against your whole thing."

If you choose to kill, I can just take what I did before in exchange. No harm, no foul as you say.

I was prepared for this, but the rage is so difficult to contain, even when I knew it was coming. This bitch is not getting another of my kids from me. I can feel Gramps trying to fight the time freeze but I hope he can calm down enough to let me handle this.

"See, I can't do that," I tell her as I pick at my cuticle. "The thing is, I already swore that anyone who attempts to harm my children will meet with death. So, if you take one, I will have to try to kill you. You'll have to kill me permanently to stop me and that would mean you can't keep your word to keep me alive until I pop out a living kid. So you kinda sorta don't have the ability to get any more kids out of me now."

I can see her anger at my logic, but she knows it's true. I don't know if she knows I'm aware of how she played me, but this is just payback, bitch. It's only the start if you cost me anything else. Ask anyone who knows me, I don't stop until I get my revenge.

Very well, my child. I shall handle this princeling and you and your family shall leave to home and be safe from any repercussions from this one time.

She is visibly clenching her teeth through that promise. Oh, wow. I did not expect to piss off a Goddess and get away totally scot-free, but if it happens today, I'll take it.

"Much appreciated, G Lady. Pleasure doing business with ya." I give her a bow of my head and when she restarts time and turns to face the prince, I flip her the bird with both hands. I can hear choked sounds and gasps of surprise. I don't know if it's because she suddenly appeared to them or if they saw me. Either way, I'm smiling wide now.

"Who are you to interfere in the ways of the Faerie kingdom of the Eastern Unseelie?" the idiot prince dude demands of the freaking Goddess.

WHO AM I?

She starts to grow until she is as tall as the room and glowing brighter than the fake sunlight coming in the windows.

WHO ARE YOU TO TRY TO TAKE WHAT IS NOT YOURS? WHO ARE YOU TO USURP THE WILL OF A GODDESS? YOU DARE CLAIM WHAT IS MINE AS YOURS!

I think the prince just shit his pants. The other ogres have gone, but Edith stayed with us. I like her a lot. She's like that cool auntie who looks like she'll be all strict but will feed you candy and stuff. I've never had one, but I've seen it on tv. The more I think about it, the I've seen it on tv thing is showing me just how messed up my life really was growing up.

I feel bad for Felix though as I look around the room some more. I don't think he's gotten up from the cold hard floor once since he dropped down earlier. He's been through an awful lot today, what with the head wound and then getting bossed around by all of the alpha males here. He's gotta come back home with us. He needs to be somewhere where I can teach him the art of managing alphas. I think I'm pretty good at it.

I should probably be paying attention to the argument going on, but I don't care. I played my trump card and won today. It may not work next time, but for now we all get to go home. Tucking myself into Daddy's side, I just try to make sure I keep my thumb out of my mouth until we get back to the car.

Ric

I knew from Ethan's memories that he has had actual conversations with the Goddess before, but today takes the cake. I never thought I would be in her presence, let alone get to witness her tear down a fae prince. I hate that yet another person has a public claim on my boy, but whatever keeps him safe is fine with me at this point. The anger and jealousy I used to show without hesitation aren't helping anyone, and the most important thing is that he is here in my arms, where he belongs.

The drive back home from Atlanta takes a few hours. Ethan wanted to stop in and visit the World of Coke before we left, but the rest of us wanted to get as far away from there as possible. Maybe in a few years we can come back and visit, if Prince Kestion grows up a bit. Apparently his little bit of sightseeing over the summer before his flight is what brought him back on the fae's radar. He was spotted when he was here.

Felix and Edith are both coming back with us. Edward has invited Edith to his property on the coast. Apparently, she's a type of royalty herself. Kestion was forcing her people to serve him and his lackeys due to some debt of her father's. He called her debt cleared when she requested to leave with us. That set her and every one of the ogres in the city free. I don't think it will be long before he finds himself with no ogres left in Atlanta.

Felix is going to move in with his sister wherever she decides to call home. They are welcome in the Jameson pack and I'm sure both Bennet and Edward will offer places for them as well. We all seem to feel the same way. Wherever Ethan's friends want to be, they are welcome. Well, at least once we figure out the Connor and Shaun situation, anyways. That's going to be interesting to figure out.

We're still about an hour away from home when I notice the memory taking over my vision. I tap Max on the shoulder to signal him what is happening and he nods. It might have been months since he's sent me a memory, but he's been very stressed lately. It's understandable.

The memory isn't a long one. In fact, it's just a bunch of short clips thrown together. Now I understand what Shaun was blowing up about, what Edward and Bennet both figured out. I feel kind of dumb that I didn't catch on, but I'm so excited. Ethan will be an excellent papa and I'll be the best dad I can be. I just have to do the opposite of what my father did and I shouldn't screw up too bad.

"You're already the best Daddy," my boy whispers, still cuddled into my side with his eyes closed.

"Go ahead and sleep some more, baby," I say as I kiss him on top of his head. "It takes a lot of energy to grow two additional people."

Felix nearly swerves off the road and Max and I both growl at him.

"Sorry! Sorry!" he says as he clenches the wheel with both hands. "Twins are great. Twins are special... It's a really good thing Prince Kestion didn't know about this, though."

We all stare at him until he answers. Maybe we should have someone else take over driving?

"Twins in the fae are considered a curse to them... power split between two and all. One twin is supposed to kill the other, absorbing their power. Most who are at least somewhat merciful would rather kill them in the womb than force them to fight or choose death when they're older. Some kill the second born immediately upon birth so the babe never knows they had a sibling."

"Is that why Celeste wants to run?" my boy asks in a whisper. "She doesn't want to kill you, ya know. She loves you even if you are a big dummy."

Felix smiles at him through the mirror. "And I love her. But yes, that's part of it. We don't have to kill each other since we're dirty blood, but those who want to own her would make her. Alucard was only one of many who wish to take my sister's hand... most don't care to ask what she wants."

Before anyone else can comment, my boy growls before it breaks into a yawn. "Then those guys can end up same as Al did. I don't fuck around when it comes to my family."

He quickly drops back into snoring. My Blue can still fall asleep anywhere.

Getting back to the house, I carry him in through the garage and up to our room. I haven't been able to sleep in here since he left, but now it finally feels right again. I lay him down on the bed and just watch him sleep for a few minutes. I need to go get Mr. Whiskers from the car, but don't want him out of my sight again... not this soon.

Before I even finish turning around, I see Max in the doorway with the teddy and tiger in his hands.

"Figured he can hang on to Tony for little man until he's back from the cabin," he says as he brings both over to the bed. I watch as he places one on each side of Ethan and then leans down to say something in his ear. I don't hear it. If I didn't know better, I might think Max was trying to just give him a kiss on the cheek, but no. That would never happen.

Laying down in the bed next to my boy, I notice the date on the bedside clock. March 16. Huh... Well Happy Birthday to me. My boy is back home. I'm going to be a father. I think life is going to be good from now on… well once we figure out how to fix the situation with our friends…

But we have time for that. My boy has forever. Hopefully my kids will too. I lay on my side and place my hand on my boy's abdomen… twins. I hope they have his light and heart and strength. In fact, I hope they get nothing at all from me, unless it comes straight from my mother.

Listening to my boy's snores, I sit up and pull out my phone. It's time to make sure we're ready for the changes this is going to bring to us all. I start looking up therapists who specialize in trauma and relationships for supes. Maybe if I go, he'll go…

EPILOGUE

Unburied

Max

Walking out of that room and leaving Ethan in Ric's arms is probably the most painful thing I've had to do in a long time. I thought I had accepted the fact that they are mates, but apparently I lost sight of it over the last month.

I'm still pissed at Ric for how he reacted to Ethan's episode back then. I'm sure I would have noticed something more was off if I wasn't thrown off my game by Joshua, Sully, whatever his name is. Fated mate or not, Ethan is the one I love. Ethan is my reason for living and has been since he showed up in my life over a decade ago. I can't give him up again... but it hurts so much to see him with Ric, who doesn't even appreciate what fate has given him.

Climbing on my bike, I take off for a ride through the mountains. I'll get Jack from Shaun's cabin tomorrow. For today, I need the wind on my face to get rid of the tears that I can't hold back anymore. Tomorrow, I can be there for Jack. Tomorrow, I can be there for the babies.

For today? I need to be selfish.

Is my cousin safe?

This isn't the voice I need in my head right now. I send back an affirmative and build up the wall inside my mind. Being around the vampire king for the last month helped a lot for blocking. Mate or not, I want to be alone... If I can't have Ethan, I don't want anyone.

ABOUT THE AUTHOR

I am a dog mom living it up in the insanity that is Northeast Ohio. When I'm not documenting the exploits of the characters in my head, I'm either binge reading the works of other amazing authors or losing my voice at hockey games. I'm horribly addicted to coffee, anime, and Asian dramas in addition to building my ever-growing stuffie army.

To break it down to the basics, I am a neurospicy aceflux demirom hetero cis woman middle who writes about people (mostly LGBTQIA+) finding love and purpose through unexpected means. Almost all of my stories involve some facet of BDSM, but the heart of the matter is the characters and their growth.

K.A. Bauer is the paranormal alter ego of Kate Bauer. I guess you could say Kate lives in this reality while K.A. is in a reality where mythical creatures and magic exist and fate makes finding true love easier.

For links to all of my socials and to sign up for my newsletter, check out my linktree at https://linktr.ee/authorkabauer

I can be found on most social media sites under the username @authorkabauer

K.A. BAUER BOOKS

Alpha's Little Psycho Series
Alive
Holly Jolly Psycho (Novella)
Unburied
Afraid
Complete Series Omnibus

Jameson Pack Series
Fated Mistake
Doctor Mate
Half Mate
Learned Fate

All of my books that are not under an exclusivity clause are also available direct from my store
www.authorkabauer.shop

KATE BAUER BOOKS

Manor Drive Series

A Little Discovery

Drag Me Up

Pet Project

Teddy Tea Time

Night Shift

No Pain, No Gain

Wrenshaw University Series

Freshman Fifteen

Injured Reserve

Professor's Pet

Too Many Men

MR DRAG Series

Wish Upon DeStarr

PREVIEW

Afraid

Ethan

It takes me a few moments to figure out where I am when I wake up. The events of the last few months have made life a bit unpredictable. I went from being an unwanted bastard orphan to being the son of an Alpha and grandson of a vampire king... Oh and let's not forget that I'm also part fae, an omega, and fucking pregnant...

WITH TWINS!

As if my life wasn't difficult enough so far, let's just add in another major fucking obstacle to any chance of me ever being happy. Every single time I think I might be able to finally let go and just be happy, fate goes and just flips the bird and rips it all away again.

First, my mother dies in childbirth. Apparently, I was fucking up people's lives before I was even born to the point I managed to take out the *one* person who is supposed to love me without a reason to. Then, I'm given to a sadistic bitch who let me believe that she was my mother. I spent thirteen years of my life trying to get a single smile from her, a single word of praise...anything but contempt and violence...

As if that wasn't bad enough, practically the entire pack tried to kill me from the time I was in kindergarten, maybe earlier. I don't really remember. All I know is that as long as it could be ruled an accident, no one got in trouble for hurting me. None of the adults stopped it. Most of the other kids ignored it. I was so happy to get my wolf because at least with him, there was a way to escape if I ever got up the courage...

But then I was kidnapped and sold to a lab. I used to think my Uncle Carl did it for the dickwad that was our Alpha, but no... that wasn't the case. He did it for money. Alpha Richard wanted to give me to the fae to save his own ass cuz he couldn't keep it in his pants and was cut out of the deal and fucked over when Uncle Carl sold me for fifty grand to some asswipe in rural Ohio for experiments.

How fucked is that? I was sold off like an old vase. Actually, old vases are treated better than I was during transport... But people died because of that night, not like it mattered to the assholes who bought and sold me. They just wanted their money, their freedom. I almost wish those selfish pricks hadn't died so that I could get some sort of revenge...

We survived. We have mate. We have pups.

I don't want to hear my wolf right now. Yeah. I survived. I *always* survive. I can't die unless I lose my heart or my head completely. Yet another thing to curse my existence...

I stare at the ceiling of the bedroom I share with Ric and wish, not for the first time, that I had died in that lab... and stayed dead. If I had, everyone would be happy. No one would be worried or scared...

I wouldn't be terrified...

I've started feeling the little flutters in my belly. They're real now. I can't pretend anymore. I have two lives inside of me that are going to depend on me to keep them safe. But I am going to leave them even though I don't want to. My mother died in childbirth. My grandmother died in childbirth. It's going to happen to me, too. I just know it.

Ric isn't ready to be a father by himself just yet. I need to make sure everything is ready for them all to get by without me. I really don't want to leave, but...

My hand brushes the scar on my throat that still hasn't completely healed. I have the feeling it's not going to ever go away. There's something about my being pregnant that allowed me to scar, I'm sure of it. The papercut from three days ago hasn't healed. I don't heal correctly when I'm pregnant...

My phone rings and snaps me out of my thoughts. I can hear Ric curse from downstairs. I can only imagine he meant to either turn off my ringer or take my phone down with him to his office. Looking at the screen, I see it's Shaun calling. I answer so that Ric doesn't think I'm still asleep and I'll get at least some privacy for this conversation. After I say hello, I hear the click of the office door closing... yep, privacy.

"Hey, E-man," Shaun says softly. He's been gentle with me these last two months. I still can't bring myself to go into the hospital after everything that's happened, so he's had to rely on only his witchy senses to help me with my pregnancy.

"How are the twins doing today? Any weird cravings yet?"

I think about it and realize that aside from the one or two days of morning sickness, the flutters are the only real symptom I've had. Hearing that, Shaun seems to be happier than he was when he first started talking. Even though he's acting as my baby doctor, I want to talk to my best friend, so I change the subject to one that will get attention off of me.

"How's my brother treating you? Still waking up to presents on the porch?"

I had to miss the fireworks, but my best friend and my big brother discovered they're fated mates. Shaun apparently rejected Connor, but my brother is being stubborn, rightly so... I want my family whole and together and happy when I'm gone.

My voice barely wobbles as I continue the conversation, listening to my bestie going on and on about how he doesn't need another carcass or fur or blanket or groceries or anything else from my brother. It's been over six weeks and Connie's wolf seems convinced he can win over his mate while Connie himself is turning into a hermit.

Hanging up the call after about an hour of useless chit chat, I decide to go to my playroom down the hall. I'm not feeling particularly little lately, especially as my belly grows, but I want to cuddle with more than Mr. Whiskers and get away from being a grownup for a while. No one questions me or expects anything of me when I'm in my playroom. Only my stuffies know how I really feel about it all.

Ric

Something has been bothering my boy since he came back, and it's only getting worse. My Beta is in a state of mourning over his mate while his wolf is still attempting to court them. My head warrior disappears regularly, coming back more and more reserved and angry each time. Even my little brother is more emotional than usual.

Ever since our parents died, Jackie has been surrounded by me, Connor, and Max. We are the constants in his life... his whole life...

In the last year, since we found out Ethan was alive, everything has changed. We added Ethan, and Jack practically worships him. But since we got him back this time and started preparing for the twins, it's like a cloud of fear has settled on everything.

I'm terrified of losing my mate. I can't forget the fact that his healing doesn't work when he's pregnant. I asked Bennet about it last month when Ethan got a splinter that took over three hours to heal. He's just as clueless as I am. The curse, or blessing, has never fallen on an omega so we're in uncharted territory. The only theory we have is that the healing is split between father and babies since they cannot protect themselves.

All of us are looking into it, researching everything we can. I've even gotten over my aversion to Edward... mostly. The healing thing might be vampire related after all and we can't leave any stone unturned. The vampire said he'll look into it and get back to us. That was three days ago, and I'm just pacing in my office waiting for the phone to ring, like I've been for two and a half days.

A phone does ring, breaking the silence, but it's coming from our bedroom.

Shit... I forgot to grab Ethan's phone. He's supposed to be resting and relaxing according to Shaun. Until we can get him to do an ultrasound, we can only rely on Shaun's knowledge and witchcraft to help keep track of the babies and Ethan's health.

Before I manage to exit my office, I hear my boy answer the phone. He sounds like he's fully awake, so I decide he should enjoy his conversation. With Connor and Max being absent so much and Jack still in school for the next few weeks, Ethan needs a bit of interaction aside from me.

Turning back towards the desk, I feel my phone vibrate in my pocket. I pull it out and see "Gramps the Vamp" on the screen... My boy got into my phone again...

"Gimme a second, Edward," I say as I answer, still chuckling. I listen for a second out in the hallway to make sure my boy is still on the phone before I close the door to my office. This needs to be a private conversation. I don't want to worry my bluebird if I don't have to.

"Ok, we've got privacy," I tell him when I've settled into my desk chair.

"I've been looking into it, but vampire omegas are extremely rare, so we don't have much to go on," he starts off with a sigh. This isn't looking up. I don't like not knowing the dangers my mate is facing.

"But, as my wonderful sister-in-law reminded me, it's not only omegas that give birth," he adds with a chuckle. "Female vampires need to *suspend* their immortality in order to conceive apparently. This makes them as vulnerable as humans while they are pregnant according to her. This is also why you never see a pregnant vampire ..."

My brain falters for a moment while I try to compute what he's saying. If it's his vampire blood halting his healing, how in the hell am I supposed to protect him? He would never let me lock him away for his own safety.

"... as Seamus discovered, it doesn't really help."

I missed something more to the story and have to ask him to repeat himself. As I thought, vampires don't like to be coddled and it would definitely create an issue with my mate. We end up going back and forth for over two hours trying to come up with ways to protect Ethan without smothering him, and in the end it doesn't even matter.

Ethan will always do whatever he thinks is best for everyone but himself. Our biggest challenge is going to be to get him to remember the babies before he acts on anything...

I am finally able to leave my office after another hour. I had to sign off on all of the financial stuff that Connor usually handles. My Beta had better get his act together soon... especially before the babies get here. I'm not going to be an absentee father like mine was just because my best friend can't figure out his romantic life.

Once I reach the top of the stairs, I can pinpoint that my boy is in his playroom. I hear him talking to his stuffies. It's been a while since I've seen my little boy Blue come out to play and I can't fight the grin that starts to spread on my face. I didn't realize how much I miss being Daddy...

"They don't need to be scared like me so you gotta promise me you won't tell Daddy or Max or Connie or even Jackie, okay guys? Bertie, I'm talking to you, too!"

I stop just outside the door. He hasn't noticed my approach at all. My heart is splintering into a million pieces... he's afraid...

Now the question is, what is he afraid of? Is it the same fear I have for his healing? Or does he know something I don't?